HAUNTED

HAUNTED

Patrick Wallace

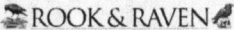
ROOK & RAVEN

First published in the United States of America in 2025
by
Rook & Raven Press

ISBN 979-8-9999800-0-7 (paperback)
ISBN 979-8-9999800-2-1 (hardcover)
ISBN 979-8-9999800-1-4 (ebook)

This is a work of fiction. Names, characters, businesses, places, events and
incidents are either the products of the author's imagination or used in a
fictitious manner. Any resemblance to actual persons, living or dead, or
actual events is purely coincidental

Cover art © 2025 Arlen Monroe
Author photo © 2025 Jen Greer Photography

Printed in the United States of America

For all the dogs that bring a little light into this world.

CHAPTER 1

E llie Hawthorne walked to campus on a patchwork quilt of fallen leaves. Neat rows of proud sugar maples lined the perimeter of the Taconic University quad, their leaves blazed like fiery orange beacons, heralds for the winter to come. It was the first truly cold morning of October, and the sky above the valley now glowed a few shades darker than it had in July.

The fourth floor of the Howard P. Jackson Building was a ghost town compared to the cacophony of the university quad. Ellie unlocked the door to her office at the end of the hall. Bold block letters stenciled across the door read: *Assistant Professor Elizabeth Hawthorne, Department of Physics*. The mailbox beside the door held a few late assignments, advertisements for upcoming conferences, and a white letter stamped with the logo of the American Physical Society. She felt a rush of adrenaline and butterflies flittered in her stomach as she collected the letter. The envelope was light in her hand, but its contents weighed heavy on her mind. The future of her career in academia hinged upon the words hidden within the confines of a thin white paper shell.

The office was small and simple, a typical workspace for a new and promising faculty member. A single window offered a pleasant view across the quad, the rolling Taconic Mountains looming beyond. With a neck craned at an awkward angle, one could even make out a sliver of the west branch of the Pematuck River as it wound its way through Brookhaven's center.

The walls were bare save for two framed photos. In one photo, Ellie stood dressed in full academic regalia, her arm wrapped around her Aunt Shirley and proudly displaying a newly acquired diploma. Aunt Shirley was the only family member who attended her graduation, and the only one she had cared to see. The diploma now collected dust in a storage box at the bottom of her closet. The robe and tam were long lost to the Salvation Army donation box.

The second photo on the office wall was of her dog Hux. A blue-mottled heeler posed with a green tennis ball on a warm summer day.

Ellie dropped her bag on the floor and took a seat behind the desk. She turned the letter over in her hands and contemplated its contents, as if with enough focus and willpower she could sway its message to her favor. So long as the letter remained sealed, its outcome was indeterminate, like a superimposed quantum wave.

A knock came from the doorway. Ben Wilson leaned against the doorjamb with both hands in his pockets. "Whatcha got there?" he asked with a wide grin.

A smile crossed Ellie's lips as she stood to greet him. "It's good to see you, Ben. This place was barely tolerable while you were away."

"Well, I guess I better think twice before I accept another guest lecturer post," Ben said in a playful tone as he stepped into her office.

Ellie gave him a warm hug. She held the embrace just a little bit longer and tighter than she normally would with a colleague.

"I see you didn't open yours yet either." Ben pulled a folded envelope from his back pocket and held it between his middle and index finger.

A twinge of sorrow hit Ellie and her smile faded as a flash of light reflected off Ben's ring finger. The gold band was a reminder of the limit of their relationship. Ben had a few years on her; he grew up with synthesizers and acid wash jeans while she rocked out to Green Day in JNCOs, but their age difference wasn't quite enough to be scandalous. The fact that he was married, though, meant he was off limits.

Ellie forced a smile. "A letter means good news, right? They wouldn't waste money on paper and ink if they weren't giving us the grant." Her tone was both playful and full of hesitant hope.

"Only one way to find out. Shall we?" Ben positioned his finger and thumb at the envelope's corner, poised to tear it open. Ellie picked her letter up off the desk and did the same so they could be opened simultaneously.

She ran a finger along the lip of the envelope and gingerly slid the letter out, then unfolded the paper to read. Ben ripped his envelope open like a wild animal and managed to tear an edge off the letter in the process. He held the two pieces together as best he could. The office was silent as the two of them took in the contents of the grant decision.

Ben broke the silence first as he read the guts of the decision aloud. "We regret to inform you..." he said. He paused for a moment and nodded as he stared at the two pieces of paper before him.

Ellie's stomach turned. Those five words were all she needed to hear. The rest of the letter was fluff, but Ben continued to read the words aloud anyway. "The American Physical Society will not be funding your proposal at this time. Unfortunately, we receive numerous high-quality research proposals every year and..."

Ellie tuned Ben's voice out as he continued to read. That was it. The last chance to fund her lab through the next semester had fallen through. No funding meant no research, and no research meant no tenure. She could feel tears start to build in the corners of her eyes and she looked up at the ceiling in a vain attempt to hold them back. It took the resolve of a Buddhist monk to stop herself from screaming out.

Ben finished reading the letter. He crumpled the paper into a tight ball and put on a dramatic show as he tossed it into the wastebasket. He sat down in one of the chairs in front of Ellie's desk, crossed his arms, and leaned back in the seat. "It's bullshit, Ellie. They wouldn't know a good proposal if it bit 'em on the ass."

Ellie collapsed into her own chair behind her desk and buried her head in her hands. She stayed silent as she struggled to maintain composure.

Ben reached across the desk and placed a hand on her

arm. "Hey, it'll be all right. Don't let the bastards grind you down."

"No, it won't be," Ellie said as she wiped her eyes.

"You've got residuals, right?" Ben asked. "Other funding sources that can keep you afloat?"

Ellie let out a deep breath and paused as she grounded herself. "It's not enough. I can keep the lights on, sure, but I can't afford beam time, let alone pay any of my students."

Ben picked a stapler up off Ellie's desk and fidgeted with it in his hands. "It'll be okay, Ellie. The university won't pull the plug just because of a small gap in funding. Your students can teach for the semester and focus on writing. Then when you get funded again you can pick it all back up right where you left off. What other proposals do you have out right now?"

Ellie looked at her calendar. It was a performance. She knew exactly which proposals had been submitted and had memorized the decision dates for each one. "The DOE grant is next; the decision should come in January or February at the latest."

"See, that's not so bad. You could be funded before summer," Ben said. He set the stapler back down on the desk, a subconscious gesture that said the awkwardness of providing emotional support had come to a close.

Ellie nodded. She knew Ben wanted to be helpful and supportive, but his reassurances weren't what she needed. What she did need was to go home, have a warm cup of tea, hug her dog, and forget about the academic grind, even if only for a few hours.

"Thanks, Ben," she said with a smile. "You're right, it'll

be okay. I appreciate you trying to cheer me up, but I need to get through the seven stages of grief in my own time."

Ben chuckled. He slapped his hands on his knees and stood. "All righty then, just give me a holler as soon as you get to the acceptance stage."

"What about your lab, Ben? I've been so wrapped up in my own funding issues I didn't even think to ask."

"Oh, don't worry about me, we still have—"

Ellie's phone rang, its shrill tone cutting off Ben mid-sentence.

"Hold that thought." Ellie raised one finger to Ben as she picked up the phone. "Hello, Professor Hawthorne speaking."

There was some background noise on the other end of the line, then a familiar voice broke through. "Professor Hawthorne, this is Alice Schwartz from the Physics Department office?" Alice phrased the words as a question, as if Ellie might not remember a woman she had spoken with at least once per week for the past two years. "There's a man here asking if he can see you, but I'm not sure if you're holding office hours right now. If you are, I can send him up."

"Who is he? A student?" Ellie asked.

Ben gestured toward the office door and mouthed "I'm leaving." Ellie smiled and waved goodbye. Ben waved back and slowly shut the office door on his way out.

"No, not a student. It's David Washington from the Society of..." There was a pause, and Ellie heard mumbling in the background from the other side of the call. "He's from the New England Paranormal Research Society... Oh wait, he says he's the *president* of the Society."

Ellie furrowed her brow. She was caught off guard by Alice's words. "Did you say *paranormal* research?"

There was more mumbling in the background. "Yes, David Washington from the Paranormal Research Society."

"Can you put him on?" Ellie asked.

Rustling static came through the speaker as the phone changed hands, then a man spoke from the other end of the line. His voice was deep and smooth. "Hello, Professor Hawthorne?"

"This is her. Did I hear right? You're from a paranormal society?"

"You heard right. My name is David Washington, I'm president of the New England Paranormal Research Society. I have an opportunity I'd like to discuss with you. A research opportunity, I mean. I'm hoping you have a few minutes to meet with me. Sorry about the late notice."

Ellie paused for a moment as she digested the words, then realized what had caused the confusion. "Mr. Washington, I think you may have the wrong person. I do *physics* research, not *psychic* research."

"I know, I know," David said. "It may seem out of the ordinary, but trust me, you're the person I'm looking for. I need a physicist for an upcoming investigation. You came highly recommended by Dr. Weiss from Columbia. I think you know him from your time there?"

As soon she heard Weiss's name, all the pieces fell into place. Ellie's old thesis advisor had been dipping his toes into the paranormal as a skeptic and science advocate for decades now. He even appeared in a few television specials while Ellie worked in his lab. "Oh boy, do I know Dr. Weiss.

Indulging in paranormal investigations may have been a pastime for him, but it isn't for me. I think he's the one you would want for your investigation."

"You're right. He is the one I want, but he dropped out a few days ago. He referred us to you as a replacement. He spoke very highly of you."

As flattering as a recommendation from the great Henry Weiss was, Ellie couldn't help but be annoyed. She had no desire to be roped into any pseudoscientific nonsense. She didn't have the time, but even more so, she lacked the forbearance. "I'm sorry, I have a very busy schedule, and I'm really not interested."

"Listen, we're desperate, Dr. Hawthorne. If I could just have a moment of your time to give you a pitch. We're not asking you to volunteer, there's generous compensation."

Ellie looked at the crumpled letter in the waste bin. The paper slowly expanded from the tight ball Ben had made and struggled to return to its flat form, like a haunting memory that refused to be forgotten.

"Professor Hawthorne, are you still there?" David asked.

"What kind of compensation?" Ellie asked.

"I'd really like to go over the details with you in person, but our patron has offered to make a private donation to your lab," David said.

Ellie glanced at the clock above her office door. She had about two hours until a department meeting, but she needed an escape route in case Washington turned out to be a nut, which was a likely scenario given his organization. So, she lied. "I have about fifteen minutes before I need to run to a meeting. Think you can give me the elevator pitch in that time?"

"Yes, I can work with that."

"Come up to my office, Room 408. Alice can tell you how to get here." Ellie hung up the phone and waited for David Washington to arrive.

CHAPTER 2

David arrived at Ellie's office. He wore a tweed blazer atop a maroon turtleneck sweater. A leather satchel was slung over his right shoulder. He was tall and wide built, and his stature suited his deep strong voice. Flecks of gray peppered his dark hair and short-cropped beard, and Ellie thought he bore more than a passing resemblance to Idris Elba. The age lines on his face put him in his early fifties. Between his clothing and his age, Ellie might have mistaken him for a fellow faculty member.

"Professor Hawthorne?" David asked while knocking on the frame of Ellie's office door.

"Come in."

"I'm David Washington, thanks for taking the time to meet me." He walked toward her desk with an outstretched hand.

Ellie met his hand and shook it. His grip was strong and firm, while his skin was soft and smooth. Ellie had grown up around men who worked with their hands day in and day out.

Their hard and unforgiving labors were reflected in their thick and calloused skin. David had the hands of a man who made a living with his mind, not with his body.

"Of course, please take a seat, Mr. Washington." Ellie gestured to the two chairs in front of her desk that were typically reserved for students.

"Please, call me David," he said. David sat down and placed the leather satchel onto his lap. He began to undo the clasp when he noticed the two framed photos behind Ellie's desk. "Is that a blue heeler?"

Ellie smiled and turned to admire the photo. "Yeah! His name is Hux, short for Huxley, and he's the love of my life."

David let out a hearty laugh from deep in his belly. "No one else could compete, I'm sure of it. They're smart dogs. Where'd you get the name Huxley? Big fan of *Brave New World*?"

"Actually, I've never read it," Ellie said. "I named him after Thomas Huxley. He was an old school biologist, and a quote of his was what made me want to be a scientist in the first place."

David shook his head. "Never heard of him. What was the quote, if you don't mind my asking?"

Ellie opened a desk drawer and removed a book thick with earmarked pages. She opened to a pink Post-It near the beginning and read aloud. "Sit down before fact like a little child, and be prepared to give up every preconceived notion, follow humbly wherever and to whatever abyss nature leads, or you shall learn nothing."

David nodded. "Wise words."

"Well, they certainly inspired me." Ellie shut the book

and set it aside on her desk. "Anyway, I think you had a proposal for me?"

"Yes, you're right, we should get down to business. Have you heard of us before? The New England Paranormal Research Society?"

Ellie shook her head. "I'm sorry to say I haven't."

"I figured not. We research paranormal claims of all sorts, but mostly we do hauntings. It's sort of become our specialty. Speaking of..." David reached into the inside pocket of his blazer and pulled out a business card. He passed the card across the desk to Ellie. Its face was adorned with the usual contact information alongside a logo in the shape of a stylized eye.

"Have you ever heard of Bruker House?" David asked.

"Again, I'm sorry to say I haven't. Should I have?"

"No. I'd honestly be surprised if you had. I've been researching the paranormal for over twenty years now and I just heard about the house for the first time a month ago."

"It's a haunted house I assume?"

"Well, that's the story." David opened the clasp on his satchel.

The dull *snap* of the clasp echoed in Ellie's ears. She stiffened as her spine ran cold, then took a deep breath and let the moment pass. Memories that ached to be released remained hidden in their lockbox at the bottom of her mind. "Is the house here in Brookhaven?" she asked, her voice calm and collected, betraying no hint of the cold tingle that persisted on the back of her neck.

"No, it's up north in Maine, in a small town called Narramissic." David dug through the satchel's contents.

Ellie shrugged and shook her head. "I've only ever been to Portland."

"It's about an hour north of there. Not quite on the coast, but near enough," David said. He found what he had been searching for in the satchel and pulled out a manila folder stuffed with documents. He opened the folder in his lap and thumbed through pages of newspaper clippings, written reports, and photographs within. While some documents were held together with paperclips or staples, others were loose and on the cusp of an escape from their manila shackles onto the newfound freedom of her office floor. David pulled a photograph free from beneath a paperclip and slid it across the desk to Ellie.

In the sepia-toned photo, a Queen Anne mansion stood tall and proud atop a hill. It was a beautiful old home. A mansard roof encircled its crown, a single tower stood guard at the front like an obedient sentry, the windows and doors were wrapped in ornate details, stained-glass and bay windows adorned every wall. The house would be right at home in a Hollywood horror. It could stand in for the house in *Beetlejuice*, the Addams Family mansion, the Bates house, or a dozen other hair-raising on-screen homes.

"And here's a more a recent one," David said as he passed another photo from the folder.

The second photo of the house was from a slightly different angle and in full color. Although it was recognizably the same house, it seemed to have lost its sense of pride. The paint was peeling, awnings above the windows hid the ornate detailing, and several of the walls were overgrown with ivy. Trees had matured around the base, which crowded its placement on the hilltop and diminished its foreboding presence.

"It's been repainted and had some renovations done since that photo, but that's more or less how the house looks today," David said.

Ellie handed back the pictures. "How come it's always an old Victorian that people say is haunted? You guys ever investigate a raised ranch? Maybe a mid-century condo?"

David smiled. "I never really thought about it, but I guess old houses have more history. More stories to tell."

"If you believe in that sort of thing."

"Whether you believe in hauntings or not, Bruker House has an interesting history." David thumbed through more photos and documents on his lap.

Ellie looked at the clock above her door. She made sure the gesture was obvious. "On the phone you mentioned a donation?"

"I did, but if it's okay, I'd like to give you the background on Bruker House and then we can talk about compensation."

Ellie nodded and let out an exasperated sigh. "Sure."

"So, the house was built by Alexander Bruker and his wife Helena in..." David flipped a page, "1874. Alexander was heir to a timber fortune dating all the way back to the Massachusetts Bay Colony. The family up and moved from Boston to northern Maine after several failed business dealings in Massachusetts. The official story is they wanted to be closer to the family's timber tracts, which was the only profitable venture they had left. If you dig into the history though, other reasons start to peek through. Alexander's wife Helena was... Let's just say she was unpopular in Boston. She was accused of impiety, and both of them were excommunicated from their congregation at St. Elias. There's also rumors they had a child who died shortly after birth, but it's difficult to confirm in the public record. Their life in Maine seems relatively uneventful until Helena's death in 1889. In the decade after, timber profits began to wane, and Alexander died as a recluse in 1903."

David flipped through the folder on his lap and produced another photo. "Here they are, Alexander and Helena."

In the photo, a man and a woman stood in front of a large ornate porch that Ellie recognized as Bruker House. A mustached man and a woman with sharp features stood side-by-side without touching one another. They stared into the camera with dry, expressionless faces. Ellie always thought old photos seemed to alienate those of the past. The Brukers were real people with full lives. They had hopes and dreams, they had decades of memories full of happiness and sorrow. They laughed together, they argued, they kept secrets. The technology of the time may have captured their faces, but it failed to capture any life from these people. Their humanity was lost in the past, while what lived on in black-and-white was nothing but a shadow, a ghostly visage.

"Cute couple," Ellie said. She handed back the photograph and David slid it back into its home in the folder, secured beneath a paperclip, buried amongst decades of long-forgotten history.

"The real story isn't about Alexander and Helena though. I can't find documentation that anything out of the ordinary occurred during their stay in the house, not that's been recorded anyway. What's really interesting is what happened to the occupants after them."

David slid his finger down a document in the folder as he read through the lines. "Since Alexander and Helena had no children, the estate was inherited by Alexander's nephew, James Bruker. James moved his wife and two children into the home in 1905. Two months after they arrived, their youngest daughter Mary disappeared. She was only three years old. Several searches were organized with the local community, but the Brukers never found her. Later that same year, James himself disappeared. The rumor at the time was he left his family behind, grieving over his loss of Mary. Although some folks said he ran off with another woman. These were only the first two in a long history of unexplained disappearances at Bruker House.

"James's widow and remaining child moved out of the home to live closer to her family in Connecticut. The house was left in the care of a groundskeeper by the name of Edward Larson. He didn't live there, but he was on the grounds often for upkeep and maintenance. Edward cared for Bruker House for three years until his own disappearance in 1909."

"I see a pattern here," Ellie said.

"And it keeps on going. There have been eleven disappearances in all."

"They never found any sign of these people? No bodies?"

David shook his head. "Nothing. The house changed hands six times over the next century. Two families took up full-time residency, and both left after a family member vanished within the first year. Believe it or not, other than the original owners, there have been no recorded deaths at the house."

David flashed a few photos. An older man wearing a Shriner's fez, a woman at the beach, a young girl with a black eye sitting on a bed. "All of them gone without a trace. The most recent disappearance was Lizzy Aldrin in 1982." David showed a photo of a girl of high school age. Her blonde feathered hair framed a bright and youthful smile.

"Aside from the disappearances, there have been dozens, maybe even hundreds of stories and eyewitness accounts over the years. All manner of strange events and sightings at Bruker House. I have the most famous ones documented here." David tapped the thick manila folder with his finger. "But I figure the anecdotes wouldn't interest you. The missing people, though, are undeniable."

"And no one has disappeared since 1982?" Ellie asked.

"Right. Although, the house has been vacant since '82, so there hasn't been much opportunity. It remained under the ownership of Lizzy's father Jason Aldrin until his death this past year. He refused to let anyone onto the property."

"So why investigate the house now, forty years later?"

"Well, after Aldrin died, the house was bought at auction by a man named William Warwick. He's the one who reached out to us to investigate the paranormal nature of the house, and the one offering to make a donation to your lab should you decide to join us."

David closed the folder and set it on the chair beside him. He leaned forward in his seat and placed his elbows on his knees, his fingers loosely interlaced in front of him. "You see, Mr. Warwick is interested in turning Bruker House into a tourist attraction. He thinks it'll be the next Winchester House or Borden House, the Queen Mary maybe. A destination for those interested in the paranormal. He approached the Society last month hoping an investigation would lend credence to the paranormal claims. He's also commissioned Alaina Cross to join our team to add a little celebrity flair."

"Who?" Ellie asked.

"I'm not surprised if you haven't heard of her since the supernatural isn't really your thing. Alaina Cross is pretty famous in the paranormal investigation world though. A clairvoyant with a weekly podcast and a large social media following. I guess Mr. Warwick thought adding some star power to the investigation would be great for marketing."

Ellie nodded. "I see, and that's where Weiss came in too, I suppose?"

"Exactly. Your old mentor has become somewhat of a celebrity himself, on the other side of the spectrum, of course, following in the footsteps of James Randi, Carl Sagan, and the like. I guess Warwick and his investors felt that the investigation team was a bit too biased between a paranormal society and a famous clairvoyant. They wanted a skeptic to balance out the investigation and bring a scientific perspective. Of course, now that Professor Weiss is out... Well, here I am talking to you."

Ellie shook her head and let out a sound that was half-gasp, half-chuckle. "You want me to step in for the great Henry Weiss?"

"Well, he did recommend you. With raving reviews, I might add."

Ellie pinched the bridge of her nose and shook her head

back and forth as she considered how to respond. Good old Weiss had recommended her; it was just one more stress test from her old advisor.

"Mr. Wash... David. Weiss may have been my advisor at Columbia, but that doesn't mean I can do what he did. It just isn't me. We're talking about the man who revealed Reverend Miller's faith healing hoax live on television. On the reverend's own show, nonetheless! He went toe-to-toe with Ariel Acosta on *The Tonight Show* and showed her levitating crystal illusion was nothing but a cheap carnival trick! He's been a champion for science and skepticism for decades. If you want star power, he's your guy. But me? I'm a nobody. I'm just not it."

David absorbed her words for a moment before he responded. "I hear you, I do, but he recommended you specifically out of all his students and colleagues. And to be honest, I'm kind of in a bind here since he dropped out so suddenly."

"He knew I was teaching at Taconic. I'm sure he just thought I'd be a convenient choice for you since we're in the same town," Ellie said.

"No. Not from the way he spoke. He really believes in you."

Ellie had no response.

"Listen, here's the bottom line," David said. "We plan to investigate Bruker House for three nights next week, and we'd love to have you join us as a scientist and a skeptic. I understand it's a big request, I understand it's short notice, and I understand Henry Weiss has big shoes to fill, but Warwick and his investors are putting a lot of funding into this house and into this investigation. They offered Weiss one hundred thousand dollars in funding for his participation, and they're willing to make the same offer to you if you're up for it."

Ellie's heart skipped a beat. The world slowed down and stopped to a dead halt as David dropped the number. One hundred thousand dollars was less than half of what she had asked for from the American Physical Society, but it would be enough to keep her lab running for another semester, maybe even two. All she could manage to get out as a response was, "That's a very generous offer."

"What do you think, can we count you in?"

Ellie sat in silence as she considered the proposition, then spoke her thoughts out loud. "It's a lot to take in all at once. Deciding whether or not to investigate a haunted house certainly wasn't a choice I was expecting to have to make today. The grant would be huge for my lab, but on the other hand, something like this could be viewed negatively by the school and by my colleagues. I could be seen as not taking my role in academia seriously. It could even bring a bad reputation to the university."

"Weiss has been doing this sort of thing for decades, and he's very well respected at Columbia."

"Weiss can get away with it because he's Weiss. He's been tenured since the Stone Age. He was an accomplished scientist for decades before he started debunking con men and pseudoscience. First of all, I don't have tenure, and I need to consider what a review committee would think of all this. But more importantly, Weiss is a man. Do you know how hard it is to be taken seriously as a woman in physics? It's a boy's club through and through, and I already have an uphill battle to fight to prove myself against my male peers."

David looked off to the side. "I'll admit, I hadn't considered that."

"It's not a no, it's just a lot to consider. When do you need a decision by?"

"We're driving up on Monday, so I really need something ASAP. I know it's short notice, but at least there won't be classes to work around. For Weiss's convenience, we scheduled the investigation to overlap with fall break, and I think that works out for you too."

"Classes may be out next week, but I have midterms to grade, papers to write, a lab to run. Not to mention finding someone to take care of Hux while I'm gone."

"Well, I can't help with most of that, but I'm sure we could arrange for your dog to come along. We're all dog lovers at the Society, myself included."

Ellie stayed silent as she worked out the puzzle in her mind. A one hundred thousand dollar grant without the need to justify spending or write quarterly reports. It would mean peace of mind in the coming semester for her and her students. Monday was short notice, but if she called in a few favors from her colleagues, she might be able to make it work.

David sat up straight. "I get it, I've dropped a bomb on you, and you need to think about it. Why don't you come by the Paranormal Society headquarters tonight? Alaina is flying in today to meet the rest of the investigation team. It'll be a great chance for you to meet everyone too. Maybe it'll help you make your decision."

Ellie nodded. "You're right, meeting the others might help. I can't promise anything, but I'll try to make it."

David stood and slung the satchel over his shoulder. "Okay, I think I've said my piece. Come by around eight o'clock and meet everyone if you can. The address is on the business card I gave you, and my number is on there too if you need it." He reached his hand out again to shake. "It was nice meeting you, Dr. Hawthorne."

"Likewise, and please, call me Ellie." She met his hand once again and felt his firm, smooth grip wrapped around hers.

"Oh, and you can hang onto this if you want to flip through some of the history yourself. It's all copies, so don't worry about losing it." David handed her the overflowing manila folder. The entire recorded history of Bruker House was neatly enclosed within her hand. Its secrets, however, remained buried deep within its walls, aching to be set free.

CHAPTER 3

Thunderheads rolled in from the west and swept over the Pematuck Valley. The deep blue October sky that hung above Brookhaven was replaced by a dark gray blanket as evening fell. Streetlamps burned with a deep amber glow that gave the illusion of warmth in the cool crisp autumn air.

Ellie drove along the river, past the rows of brick warehouses which lined its banks, remnants of a time since passed when rivers were highways and industry was built on hydropower. She turned into a small post-war neighborhood known locally as Hobb's End, an area that local teens affectionately called Hobgoblin's End.

Strobes of lightning flashed in the distance, and thunder, still soft, teased an impending torrent. The trees lining the street waved and swayed in the wind. The few leaves that still clung to their homes amongst the branches relented and joined the storm on its march east.

The address on David's business card led to a small craftsman bungalow on the corner of Van Buren and

Seventh. Ellie parked along the curb in front of the house as the first few raindrops splattered against the windshield of her Wagoneer. A small wooden sign hung above the front porch steps and swayed in the wind. In the dim evening light, Ellie could just make out black lettering burned into the wood which read: *The New England Paranormal Research Society, Est. 1996.*

Raindrops beat against the roof of the Jeep, an occasional hail stone punctuating the rhythm like a rim shot in a drum line. Ellie cracked open the Wagoneer's door and maneuvered her umbrella through the gap. A strobe of lightning flashed and was shortly followed by a crack of thunder. She left the Jeep and hurried toward the bungalow and up the porch steps. A large picture window at the front of the house showed men and women seated within. Logs blazed in the fireplace and bathed the room in a flickering orange glow. On the porch, Ellie shook the rain from her umbrella, and the door cracked open just as she prepared to knock.

"Ellie, I'm glad you could make it!" David said. A large smile crossed his face. He shuffled to the side of the doorway as he gestured for her to come in. "Please, make yourself at home. We're all sat down in the parlor."

"Good to see you again too," Ellie said as she walked through the door.

Like many old homes, this house had its own distinct smell. Layers of aroma accumulated in a house over the decades, the wood of the frame and the floors, the iron of old radiators, smoke and ash from the fireplace. Decades of oils and fragrances steeped in its very walls. Smell was a part of the story told by a home. Stories of the people who spent time there, and the things that they held dear. This old home smelled of pine and leather, with light smoky undertones. Its smell was warm and welcoming.

"Here, let me take that. I'll hang it on the mantel to dry." David took the wet umbrella from Ellie's hand and led her into the parlor.

The walls of the room were paneled with dark wood, a single large window was pelted by rain and hail. The center-piece of the room was a stacked stone fireplace in which a modest fire now crackled. The fireplace was flanked on either side by two large walnut bookcases stacked with old leather-bound tomes and antiques and curiosities of all kind. Ellie saw old scientific instruments and taxidermies, objects carved out of stone and wood, dolls, photographs, and even a rusty old lunchbox.

Three strangers sat beside the glowing fire.

An elderly man with a bushy white beard lounged in an old leather armchair beside the fireplace. A chair fit for old men to smoke cigars and drink whiskey as they rattled on about politics.

His fingers were interlaced across a protruding belly. Ellie thought that come December, he must avoid the color red, lest he be pestered nonstop by children who've mistaken him for Santa Claus.

Beside the old man, two women sat beside one another on a sofa. One woman was middle-aged with curly hair and sharp prominent features. She wore a strapless green dress and held a matching clutch in her lap. She looked as if she belonged at a fancy cocktail party instead of a ghostbuster meet and greet.

The second woman sat on the opposite end of the sofa. She was much younger, college-aged at most, and had the most striking appearance of the three. She had long jet-black hair that draped over her shoulders and spilled over her chest in sharp contrast with her ghost-like pale skin. She wore loose, flowing black clothes, accented by black nails, a choker, and heavy eyeliner. The woman looked as though she had stepped out of a black-and-white movie, save for the radiant red of her lipstick. She held both hands in her lap and absent-mindedly fiddled with her bracelet.

David crossed the room and hung Ellie's umbrella from the mantel. He threw a fresh log onto the fire, and a blast of embers shot through the damper and up the chimney. He turned around and stood in front of the fire as he addressed the room. "Everyone, this is Professor Elizabeth Hawthorne. She teaches at Taconic University. I'm hoping she'll take over for Professor Weiss and join us next week at Bruker House."

The old man in the corner raised a hand and said, "Hello." The middle-aged woman on the sofa beamed and said, "Nice to meet you." Her young black-and-white neighbor gave a silent nod with the faintest of smiles.

David gestured with an open hand to the old man. "This is Lou Thomas. Lou has worked with the Society on and off for nearly a decade now. He's an expert in demonology and is a regular on our investigations. You were a preacher for, what was it, Lou? Twenty years?"

"Twenty-two! Wrote a new sermon every Sunday." Lou stood using both arms to push himself up from the chair. He grunted and stumbled just a little as he stood. "It's a pleasure, Miss Hawthorne," he said as he held out a hand for Ellie to shake. He had a mild New England accent, and the way he pronounced "pleasure" left very little "R" to be found.

"Pleasure meeting you too," Ellie said. She met his hand and shook his firm grip. The skin of his hand was thin and loose, and moved easily across the flesh beneath.

"I believe it's Dr. Hawthorne, not Miss," the middle-aged woman on the sofa said to Lou. "She's only a professor at one of the best schools in the country after all." Her voice was smooth and she had a mild accent that Ellie couldn't quite place. It had a tinge of Southern, but with something else mixed in as well.

"Sorry, Dr. Hawthorne is what I meant," Lou said with a somewhat sheepish look.

"It's all right. In fact, I'd prefer if you all would just call me Ellie."

Outside, the wind howled, interrupted by growing rumbles of thunder.

"Well, Ellie, I'm Charlotte." The middle-aged woman stood from the sofa with an air of elegance and held the small clutch in front of her with both hands in a move that looked as though it had been rehearsed many times over. Ellie was surprised by the woman's height; she was easily six feet tall even without accounting for the two-inch heels she wore with the cocktail dress. In addition to her height, she was slender with a build fit for a fashion model, and judging by the outfit she wore, she knew it. She held out her hand, and Ellie shook it. Her fingers were long and narrow, and her touch soft and gentle.

"Nice to meet you," Ellie said.

"Charlotte Bertrand is a member of our sister organization down in Louisiana, the Gulf Coast Society for Paranormal Research," David said.

"I'm on loan," Charlotte said as she took her place back on the sofa and nestled the clutch into its home on her lap.

David laughed. "She's one of the foremost cryptozoologists in the country, and we're lucky to have her with us. Her expertise will help us rule out the possibility of any cryptids at Bruker House."

"Any what?" Ellie asked

"Cryptids," Charlotte said. "Animals that may exist but are unconfirmed. Think of Bigfoot, or the Loch Ness Monster, although I don't expect we'll find either of those two up in Maine." She laughed. Despite her elegant dress and movements, her laugh was decidedly informal.

David gestured to the young black-and-white woman on the sofa. "Finally, we have Alaina Cross, who's joining us all the way from L.A. Alaina is host of the podcast *The Oracle of Orange County*, and is perhaps the most well-known clairvoyant in the country."

"Hi," Alaina said. Her voice was barely more than a whisper. She lifted just a few fingers from her lap in a weak, noncommittal wave.

Ellie waved back. "Nice to meet you. You're a psychic?"

Alaina nodded and in a low breathy voice said, "I like to use the term clairvoyant."

Ellie wasn't sure what the difference was between a clairvoyant and a psychic, and she didn't have enough interest to ask. The two were both equally fictitious as far as she was concerned, and it wasn't worth digging any deeper into. She only hoped that Alaina was the kind of psychic that had fooled themselves into believing their own bullshit instead of the kind that knew full well what they were doing was a scam. "Clairvoyant, got it," Ellie said with a nod.

"And you've already met me," David said. He took a seat in a chair near the fireplace across from Lou.

"True, but I didn't get to hear your qualifications," Ellie said with an air of playfulness in her voice. She sat down alone on a second sofa across from Charlotte and Alaina.

"True. I suppose I owe myself a proper introduction. I'm president of the New England Paranormal Research Society, which I founded with a few friends back in mid-90s. I'm an Army vet, I'm a teacher, I like cold beer and lasagna, and I'm excited to investigate a haunted house next week."

Charlotte gave a few claps and Lou shouted, "Amen!"

"You teach? I would've thought you just did this," Ellie said. She gestured around at the room.

"Believe it or not, *this*," David gestured around the room, mirroring Ellie's motion, "doesn't really pay the bills. By day I teach American History at Blair Hill High School."

"Cryptozoology doesn't really pay the bills either. The paranormal is a hobby for a lot of us," Charlotte said. "I work at Lafayette Bird Sanctuary by day."

Outside, thunder clapped. Bright light strobed through the picture window, and the cozy amber glow of the parlor was interrupted by flashes of white.

"Can I ask what you teach at Taconic?" Charlotte leaned forward as she asked the question, eager to hear the answer.

"I teach Physics. My research is in high-energy physics, but I teach both General Physics in the fall and Nonclassical

Physics in the spring. My lab is studying cohesion dampening in non-temporal closed loops."

Charlotte gestured that the topic was beyond her and made a whoosh sound as she passed an open palm above her head. The elegant performance she conducted for first impressions was gradually being replaced by what Ellie assumed was the real Charlotte. "I think I understood three words of what you said."

"Sometimes I'm not sure I understand it myself. I doubt any of it is relevant to haunted houses anyway," Ellie said.

David jumped in. "We really just need a skeptic, not any specific expertise. That being said, I think your background in science could be helpful. It's our job to collect the evidence, and hopefully it'll be enough to convince you just as well as any science project."

"To be honest, if the evidence you're going to collect is a few cold spots and blurry photos of shadows on the wall, I can tell you right now you won't convince me of anything."

Charlotte furrowed her brow and tilted her head to the left. "Well, how would we convince you, cher? What would make you believe something supernatural was happening in that house?"

"Nothing will ever convince her," Lou said from his armchair. "She's already made up her mind that the supernatural don't exist and we're a bunch of frauds."

"That isn't true." Ellie turned to look Lou dead in the eye. "I always follow the evidence where it leads. I just haven't seen any good evidence for the supernatural, at least not any that can't be explained otherwise."

"You'll find some explanation for anything we find, you

folks always do," Lou said. His tone was flat, almost tired, as if he had had the same conversation a dozen times before.

"If natural mechanisms can explain something, then it wouldn't be evidence for the supernatural now, would it?" Ellie snapped back.

"Lou, I'm confident that Ellie will be skeptical, but fair," David said, hoping to make peace and ease the rising tension. He glanced back and forth between Lou and Ellie. "I don't think Ellie will be intentionally obstinate."

"No, of course not. I also want to say that even if I can't explain something, it doesn't mean I believe it's supernatural. I'm perfectly comfortable to say, 'I don't know.' I think in most cases, that's the only honest answer we can give."

Lou let out a grunt and didn't pursue the subject further.

Satisfied with Lou's response, David continued. "If the evidence we collect is enough to get you to say, 'I don't know,' well, to me that would be evidence of something out of the ordinary. Maybe not supernatural, but it would count for something."

A few flashes of lightning streamed through the window, followed by a crack of thunder, a strike close enough it could've been across the street. All five of them jumped at the sound. The crack echoed in Ellie's ears, a snap followed by a woman screaming in agony, wailing. Memories and pain demanded to flood into the forefront of her mind, but decades of denial and repression held back the deluge like a dam.

"It's really picking up out there, listen to that wind howl," Lou said.

Ellie relaxed. There was no screaming woman; it was thunder and wind, dust and shadows. The dam held.

"Well," Charlotte said, "what kind of evidence are we talking about? What might get you to say, 'I don't know'?"

As Ellie considered the question, she was acutely aware of four pairs of eyes on her, each of them eagerly awaiting a response. What *would* it take to do a scientifically valid experiment that tested for the paranormal? How could you reliably detect a supernatural presence? What would you use as a control? These were questions to which Ellie had no satisfying answer.

"You're a cryptozoologist, right?" Ellie asked Charlotte.

"Yes."

"You said you aren't expecting to find Bigfoot at Bruker House, but for a moment let's imagine you were. What evidence would you collect? How could you confidently say there is a Bigfoot?" Ellie asked.

"Well, I guess it would be just like any other wildlife survey. I would look for footprints or droppings, I would listen for calls." Charlotte looked up at the ceiling as she thought, and counted off items on her fingers one-by-one as she listed them. "I'd set up some wildlife cameras. For the most foolproof evidence, I'd need to get Bigfoot clearly on camera, or maybe even trap him, assuming I could manage a trap large enough, that is."

"Right! Real physical evidence of the thing you're looking for. A good video or an actual captured Bigfoot would be indisputable. I expect the same quality of evidence to confirm a haunting."

"Ghosts and demons don't typically leave behind footprints or droppings," Lou said.

David let out one of his deep belly laughs. "Ain't that the truth."

Ellie gathered her thoughts and laid them out for the group. "True, maybe they don't leave footprints or droppings, but they do manifest physically in some sense. People claim that ghosts are able to move objects or even be captured on camera. If I were to see video of Bigfoot on one of Charlotte's wildlife cameras, a clear high-resolution image, it would be enough for me to say, 'I don't know what that is.' It could be a man in a suit, it could be an abnormal bear; hell, depending on the footage, I may even be convinced that it's definitely Bigfoot. Likewise, if I see a ghost on camera, not just something that moved unexpectedly or a weird shadow or some other nonsense, but a real actual video of a ghost, that might be enough for you to get an 'I don't know' out of me."

David looked distraught. "Ellie, I think you need to temper your expectations a bit. Seeing a full spectral apparition like that is incredibly rare. I've been doing paranormal investigations for over twenty years, and only once in my life have I seen what you're describing. Most people in the field have never seen something like that."

"I'm one of them," Charlotte said. She raised a hand out of her lap. "I've been on dozens of investigations, I've seen all sorts of things that I can't explain, but I've never seen an actual ghost. I've never seen a cryptid either, for that matter, but that doesn't mean I don't have good reasons to believe they exist. Well...some of them anyway."

Lou jumped back into the conversation. "I seen my wife

Christie three times after she passed," he said. He glanced at everyone in the room one by one. "She's the only spirit I ever seen though."

Ellie shrugged. "I'm sorry, but for me a haunting is an extraordinary claim, and if I'm going to be convinced, it'll require extraordinary evidence."

Outside, the howl of the wind had settled, and trees returned to a gentle sway. Thunder rumbled, quieter now and more distant. Rain drops still pattered against the parlor's picture window, but the hail was a distant memory.

Alaina spoke for the first time since her introduction. It was the loudest she had spoken thus far, and if she had made eye contact instead of speaking into her lap, she may have even reached the level of a normal speaking voice. Her tone was light and airy, like a loud whisper. Ellie assumed it was a part of the identity she was selling; just like her black-and-white look, her voice was part of a performance. A character she played on a podcast. "You talk about seeing an apparition as if it's the first step to believing in the supernatural, but it's not. What would you say about a blind man who refuses to believe a lion exists until he walks into one's den to reach out and touch it? You'd call that man a fool. You'd say that by the time he reaches out to touch a lion, he'd be close enough for it to kill him. You'd plead with him to believe those who can see the lion standing there, waiting to strike. To me, you are the blind man." She looked up at Ellie, and then around to the other three. "All of you are. The amount of energy it takes for a presence to manifest itself physically is unimaginable, attainable only through great power and emotion. Seeing a full spectral apparition isn't a first step to the supernatural. It's more likely to be the last."

Alaina paused, and the room was silent. She played with her bracelet and her eyes returned to focus on her lap, but all the other eyes in the room were on her. "I can't confirm that there's a haunting at Bruker House without going there and feeling it in person, but if that house is half as tainted as they say it is, then it's a dangerous place for each and every one of you. None of you have the psychic perception needed to do an investigation like this safely. All of you are like blind men, fumbling in the darkness, looking for a lion's tail to tug on."

Alaina looked up from her lap again and made direct eye contact with Ellie. "At least the others believe the lions exist and will show some caution. They won't have their hand halfway down a throat before they realize their mistake. You, on the other hand, are a disaster waiting to happen."

Ellie looked at David. "I don't need this. If your investigation is going to be full of lectures from the peanut gallery, then I'm out." She leaned forward in her seat and looked directly at Alaina. The voice she found was terse and pointed. "Lions? There are no lions to be found. It's just a house, nothing more. It's wood and plaster and dust. And I'm sorry to say it, but I'm not impressed by your act. I don't believe in your psychic bullshit, and I think you and everyone like you is a fraud and a con artist."

Ellie stood up to leave. "David, thanks for the meet and greet. You were right, it did help with my decision. Good luck on your ghost hunt."

"Ellie, wait!" David stood as she retrieved her umbrella from its place on the mantel. "Look, I realize we don't all see eye to eye, but that's the entire point! We want to get different points of view."

Ellie nodded. "Different points of view? Well, I think we found one Alaina and I agree on. I shouldn't go. I'm sorry, but it's a no from me. This just isn't something I do. Like I told you in my office, I'm no Henry Weiss, and to be honest," Ellie looked at the other three in the room, her gaze lingering for a moment on Charlotte and the sadness in her eyes, "I don't fit in here."

"Ellie, hang on," David pleaded.

"I'm sorry, David, I can't help you." Ellie could feel the eyes staring at her back as she left the parlor, and she heard murmurs from behind as she reached the front entrance. She pulled open the heavy wooden door, and an icy wind blew in from the storm. She held her umbrella tight, and stepped from the warm orange glow of the house into the cold darkness that lay beyond the threshold.

CHAPTER 4

The rain had all but stopped by the time Ellie made it home. The streets of Brookhaven glistened in the Wagoneer's headlights. Moist air condensed into a light mist, and yellow halos glowed like auras around each streetlamp. Trees which had proudly burned that morning in brilliant oranges and reds were nearly stripped bare, their empty branches reaching toward the sky like skeletal fingers.

An earthy smell hung in the air as Ellie walked the cobbled path to her front door. Opening it, she was met with a warm welcome from Hux, and the two of them began their daily greeting ritual. She told Hux how dearly missed he was all day in a special voice reserved for pets and babies. She knelt on one knee to ruffle his cheeks and scratch his back. Hux performed his half of the routine by trying and failing to lick her face. He pressed his head into her chest and wagged his tail with such ferocity that his entire back end swung back and forth.

"If only you knew what a day I had, buddy," Ellie said with a sigh.

Once the greeting ritual was complete, Ellie dropped her bag onto the kitchen counter and removed two folders from within. The first was an accordion folder full of ungraded quizzes, late assignments, lab reports, and all manner of academic drudgery expected of a university professor. The second was the disheveled folder from David that contained every scrap of Bruker House history he could find.

Hux dropped a tennis ball at Ellie's feet and nudged it toward her with his nose.

"You may not know it, bud, but you were this close to going on a trip next week." Ellie gestured with a small gap between her thumb and index finger.

Hux listened and tilted his head as she spoke. He didn't hear any words important to a dog—treat, walk, ball, and so on. He responded with a quiet whine, which Ellie decided to take as forgiveness for ruining his trip. She picked up the tennis ball and tossed it into the living room while Hux scrambled after it.

The clock on the stove said it was 9:20, a bit late in the evening for her to start a grading party. She decided the quizzes could wait until tomorrow and she stuffed the accordion folder back into her bag.

Ellie was looking forward to forgetting all about David and the New England Ghostbuster Gang. She had had every intention of throwing the manila folder into the trash, yet the mystery of Bruker House still piqued her curiosity. The idea of a haunting, or aliens, or any other hocus-pocus didn't interest her, but eleven people really did go missing there without a trace. It was strange, she was willing to admit that much. Instead of throwing the folder away, she opened it.

Interspersed among the missing persons were dozens of reports of strange sightings at the house. A visitor in 1910 saw a strange man looking out from an upstairs window. Two children in 1934 swore the devil himself rose up out of the fireplace and commanded them to set the carriage house ablaze. A worker in 1967 was quoted as saying he heard the disembodied voice of a woman in the parlor pleading for help followed by several horrific screams. There were countless stories throughout the years, nearly all of them so patently absurd they could be dismissed offhand as lies or exaggeration. The missing people though, they couldn't be ignored. *Eleven disappearances,* she thought as she read the names in each report dating all the way back to 1905.

Mary Bruker was the first and youngest missing person, the great-niece of Alexander and Helena who had built the house. Only three years old when she was last seen alive. The oldest was a man named Bill Sanderson, who was last seen in 1943 at the ripe old age of seventy-four.

Piece by piece, Ellie organized the mess of documents in David's folder as she wrapped her head around the mystery of Bruker House. She found several documents already bundled together for one of the eleven disappearances: Julie Campbell, whose family had occupied the house throughout the 1960s. The missing persons police report was accompanied by several others for domestic violence. As a result, Julie's father Donald was a lead suspect in her disappearance. The manila folder held only one photo of Julie, buried deep in one of the police reports. In the photo, a teenaged girl sat cross-legged on a brass bed, the wall behind papered in a garish green and yellow pattern. She had two black eyes, and the pale skin of her cheeks were peppered with cuts and bruises. The police report mentioned a broken arm. Ellie heard the snap of breaking bones followed by a guttural scream. The sound tormented her as it echoed across time and space. It travelled twenty-three years from the day her father twisted her mother's arm to breaking, and arrived in her kitchen to replay once again. Ellie focused her attention on Julie and let the memory pass. It settled like a wave on the sea, back into the depths where it belonged.

The folder had no record of what happened to Donald Campbell, but Ellie was certain he lived a long and uneventful life, as abusers of women so often do.

Of all the reports, Julie's was the only one with any hint of a suspect. It's possible her abusive father had killed her and disposed of her body, but he couldn't have been responsible for the other ten missing people. In fact, it was unlikely that any single person could be responsible for all eleven disappearances. Disregarding what would be one of the strangest MOs of all time—kidnapping people of various age and gender from a single house—Ellie did the napkin math. The last disappearance was Lizzy Aldrin in 1982, seventy-seven years after Mary Bruker in 1905. If the culprit was very young when they started, say sixteen during the first disappearance, then in 1982 they would've been ninety-three years old. It was physically possible, but Ellie couldn't imagine someone in their nineties killing and hiding bodies. Although, it was still a better explanation than invoking the supernatural. Serial killers, after all, are real.

Hux picked out a spot on the couch and entertained himself with one of his chews. He was always willing to be a sounding board for Ellie, so she called out to him, "What do you think, buddy? Was it a serial killer? Kidnapper maybe?" Hux looked up for a moment and stared back at her. When he didn't hear one of his favorite words, he went back to work on his chew.

The missing people were an assortment of children, men, women, elderly, and young. In each case, the authorities searched the grounds, questioned neighbors and relatives, and posted bulletins. Despite their best efforts, there was no evidence, no arrests, and no leads. Nothing linked the victims together besides the fact that they were last seen at Bruker House. There were eleven random disappearances in one location over a seventy-seven-year period without a reasonable explanation.

Ellie packed all the documents back into the folder and pushed it away. It documented a mystery, but held no answers. She walked to the kitchen sink and filled a tea kettle with water. The clock on the stove told her it was 10:17; she knew tea would be a mistake this late, but heated the kettle anyway.

Ellie found a notebook and a pen as she waited for the water to boil. At the top of a blank page she wrote *Explanations for the Bruker House Mystery*. She made a list of bullets and filled out the top row with *single serial killer* and the second with *cult murders*. The rest of the page was disturbingly blank.

Ellie considered non-sentient physical explanations. Perhaps something about Bruker House or its grounds caused each victim to become lost or trapped. She thought of the boy in *The Orphanage*, trapped in a hidden cellar. There could be a secret room, or a sinkhole, or even a well. Ellie recalled a news story from her childhood about "Baby Jessica" who had fallen into a well. Maybe Mary Hawthorne and the others had succumbed to a similar fate. Of course, Baby Jessica had lived, but maybe whatever it was at Bruker House was well hidden. She wrote down another bullet, *injured or lost in a room, well, or other space.*

The tea kettle whistled. Ellie closed the notebook and made herself a cup of Earl Grey. She sat back down at the kitchen table and reached for the manila folder again. She found the picture of Julie Campbell and stared into the girl's vacant black and blue eyes. There was no spirit behind them, no life, no joy. *You didn't just break her bones, you broke everything about her*, Ellie thought. She recognized those eyes —they were the same ones she had in every picture from her own childhood. In every school photo, every yearbook, every candid snapshot, those same lifeless eyes shone in little Ellie Hawthorne, sometimes with black and blue highlights to boot. As Ellie stared at the photo, she knew she wanted to solve the mystery of Bruker House—not for David, not for her own curiosity, not for money, but for Julie. It wasn't fair to suffer through such torment only to have her life cut short. While the rest of the investigation team wasted their time chasing ghosts and goblins, Ellie would search Bruker House for a practical explanation. Maybe she'd find an old well in the woods, or a sinkhole in the cellar. She knew it was a stretch, but maybe one abused child could help put another's story to rest.

Ellie glanced at Hux, who was still working away at his chew. "You better be careful. If you fall down a well, I might just decide to leave you there." Hux listened and responded with a gentle wag of his tail.

She looked at the clock on the stove. It was 10:52. There was no point in digging any deeper tonight. She decided to sleep on it, and if she felt the same way in the morning, she would call David.

———————

ELLIE AWOKE to the sound of screaming. Her heart pounded in her chest and pangs of fear coursed through her body. She watched her father twist her mother's arm and snap it before she was wrenched from the dream and into the dim morning glow of her bedroom. Her mother's piercing screams still echoed in her ears; they were visceral, and they sounded real.

Ellie pushed herself up against the headboard and shielded her eyes against the sunlight that streamed through her bedroom window. Her body was drenched in a cold sweat, and her clothes clung to her skin in an unpleasant clammy embrace. She looked around the room and listened, praying she wouldn't hear another scream. Hux lay at the foot of her bed, intensely focused on the bedroom window, his ears perked.

"What is it, bud? You hear something?" Ellie whispered.

Hux glanced at her and then returned his focus to the window. Fear bloomed within Ellie. The screams *had* been real, and Hux had heard them too. She threw off the covers and walked to the window in her sweat-soaked clothes.

Across the street, a group of children played blind man's bluff. A blindfolded girl stumbled across the yard with her arms outstretched before her. Several other children teased her and dodged her flailing arms. One of the girls, a younger sister perhaps, let out a high-pitched shriek as an arm swept a bit too close for comfort.

A woman ripped open the front door of the house and yelled, "What did I say about keeping it down out here? Don't make me say it again!" The children froze, then nodded at the woman's threat. After she shut the door, they continued their game.

Ellie watched the children as they played a simple game, screaming with joy in contrast to the screaming that haunted her. Screams of agony and terror followed her, manipulated her. She dreamt of her mother often, but it had been years since she dreamt of that day, that awful brutal day. She pushed the unpleasant memories back down into the depths of her mind where she hid them like a dirty secret.

She looked down at Hux beside her. He stared back and gave a few gentle wags of his tail. His bright eyes and warm face never failed to give her comfort. She bent down and held him close. "Let's not go to that dark place today," she said. "Or ever again, for that matter."

Ellie removed her sweat-soaked clothes and showered. By the time she finished getting dressed, the memories of childhood trauma and of her dream had faded away, stowed in a psychological lockbox at the bottom of her mind. She went into the kitchen and saw the manila folder spread open on the countertop. She remembered Julie, and the lockbox in her mind opened again, just a crack. David's business card was secured to the folder with a paperclip. Ellie removed her phone from her pocket and called his number.

"Hello?" David answered.

"David, this is Ellie Hawthorne. I changed my mind. I'd like to join you at Bruker House."

CHAPTER 5

Frost crunched beneath Ellie's feet as she hauled a duffle bag across the front lawn. She nestled the bag in the back of her Wagoneer beside Hux's bed. The Jeep's engine rumbled softly, warming the cabin for the comfort of its occupants, human and dog alike.

Ellie slid behind the wheel. Her knee brushed against a pink rabbit's foot charm that dangled from the Wagoneer's key ring just as it had on the day her Aunt Shirley gifted the Jeep to her. Ellie kept the keychain and the car itself unmodified and in immaculate condition out of gratitude and respect for the woman to whom she owed so much. Everything in the Jeep was original save for the radio, which had been updated to a modern Bluetooth stereo. A collection of cassette tapes had been inherited along with the car, but as much as Ellie loved her aunt, she could only stomach so much CCR before going mad. She scrolled through her phone and picked out a playlist for the road. The Violent Femmes sang about

American music as she pulled the Wagoneer onto the street and drove north toward Maine.

The Berkshires were dream-like on the crisp autumn morning. A light layer of frost covered what leaves remained on the trees, and their bright reds and golds were hidden beneath a thin layer of silver.

Ellie loved the road. Some modes of travel were about arrival at the destination in as short a time as possible. No one really wanted to be on bus with a dozen other passengers or crammed into a small seat on a jet while engines whined. The road though. Travel on the road was a destination of its own. A third place between home and the end of one's journey. The road had its own entertainment, its own food and eating habits, its own priorities.

On Route 1, just past Waldoboro, Ellie spotted a paint-peeled and off-kilter sign which read *Cedar Mill Road, 8 Miles to Narramissic*. A large white arrow pointed left toward a lonely two-lane road. Ellie followed the advice of the decaying sign and turned inland toward Narramissic, and toward Bruker House.

David had called Narramissic a town, and he was correct in the literal sense of the word, but to Ellie, Narramissic felt less like a town and more like the memory of a town that had once been. Unlike Brookhaven, which had managed to survive or even thrive thanks to the presence of Taconic University, Narramissic had succumbed to the same slow death as so many other towns across New England before it. After the logging companies left and the mills shut down, nothing remained but a hollowed-out shell where a town used to be. Narramissic had died decades ago, the few people who still lived there just refused to acknowledge it. It was a dead town full of dead people.

The center of Narramissic consisted of a single stop sign surrounded by several vacant buildings. A dive bar called Jim's Starlight Lounge seemed to be one of the few businesses still open. As she took in what passed for a downtown, her eyes landed on a billboard that depicted a woman and a child screaming in absolute terror. Large block letters beside the image read *You'll Die Screaming*.

A car horn blared from behind Ellie and her heart lurched. A lifted pickup swerved around her and accelerated through the intersection, blasting black smoke out of the tailpipe. As he sped away, the driver gave Ellie a one-fingered salute through a cracked window. Ellie looked at the billboard again and saw the woman and child weren't screaming after all, they were laughing. The block letters read *Cancer Screening* with a MaineHealth logo on the bottom right.

"I must be losing it," Ellie said to Hux through the rearview mirror. The commotion woke him from a nap, and he was standing in the trunk, ears perked.

David had made it clear that Bruker House was difficult to get to, and the address wasn't listed on any map app as far as Ellie could find. He recommended everyone to meet just outside of town at a local seafood joint called Captain Nemo's. The general contractor overseeing the renovations at Bruker House would meet them there and lead them up the house. The restaurant had a gaudy sign out front in the shape of a smiling cartoon lobster wearing a chef's hat. Faded words beneath the lobster mascot read: *Captain Nemo's, You'll Be Hooked!*

Ellie pulled into the lot and saw the other four members of the investigation already gathered around a white panel van. She parked the Wagoneer and Hux whimpered as he peered out the window, anxious to finally escape the car. "You'll have to wait here for a few minutes, bud," Ellie said as she opened the car door.

David spotted Ellie and waved as soon as she stepped out. "Ellie, glad you made it!" The other three turned to face her as she walked toward them.

Charlotte broke the loose circle and walked to meet Ellie halfway. Ellie saw she had ditched the high heels from their previous meeting in favor of a worn pair of leather boots. Even without the heels, she was a very tall woman; only David rivaled her in height. She still wore a dress, but now it was a laid-back midi with a plaid flannel shirt thrown over it. She looked as though she could have stepped out of an early 90s teen magazine. Something with a stereotypical Gen X title like *Teenage Filth* or *Grunge Wasteland*.

Charlotte opened her arms and gave Ellie a warm hug. "I'm really glad you decided to join us, cher. The team wouldn't be whole without you." Her not-quite-Southern accent came through especially strong on the word *glad*. Charlotte pointed to Hux as he stared at them from the back of the Wagoneer. "Aw, who's your little friend back there?"

"That's Hux, want to say hello?" Ellie opened the Wagoneer's rear hatch and Hux jumped out without hesitation.

Charlotte bent down and ruffled Hux's fur, and he was more than happy to accept the love and attention. "How did you get lucky enough to come along?" she asked the dog.

"It was one of my conditions for coming up here on such short notice. Hux had to come along too."

"Two investigators for the price of one. Sounds like a bargain to me," Charlotte said with a smile.

David, Alaina, and Lou joined them at the back of the Wagoneer. The five of them, six if you count Hux, formed a loose circle.

"Nice to see you again, Miss Hawthorne," Lou said. He nodded and tipped a hat that wasn't there. Ellie noticed an unamused side-eye glance from Charlotte, but she didn't correct Lou for using the wrong title.

"Please, I prefer just Ellie."

Alaina, still dressed like a black-and-white movie star, offered no greeting. The only hint of emotion on her face was a mild look of disdain focused on Hux.

"This must be the famous Huxley," David said. He bent over and put out a hand for Hux to sniff.

"Beautiful dog," Lou said. "What is that, a German shepherd?"

"Blue heeler," said Ellie.

"She got to bring a dog?" Alaina asked, her light breathy voice as loud as she could manage. She looked at David and irritation was painted clearly on her face. "If I'd known we could bring animals, I would've brought Picatrix with me."

David was taken aback by the tone of Alaina's voice. He replied calmly, but Ellie could hear a hint of irritation in his own. "Ellie didn't have much notice of the investigation, and I made a special request to Mr. Warwick that Hux be allowed to come. If I'd known you wanted to bring a dog too, I would've asked, but I didn't know." He shrugged his shoulders.

Alaina folded her arms across her chest and rolled her eyes. To Ellie, the gesture made her look even younger than she already was, more like an angsty high school teen than a young adult woman. "Picatrix isn't a dog, he's a cat. And more than just a cat, he's my familiar. I'm going into a place like Bruker House alone and... it'd be nice to have him with me."

Ellie barely resisted the urge to roll her own eyes at Alaina's melodrama, but despite her frustration, she thought she detected an undertone of fear in Alaina's voice. Genuine fear. Ellie thought maybe Alaina wasn't just a snake oil salesman after all, maybe she actually believed in all the woo and superstition that she peddled. Alaina, more than the rest of them, seemed to be legitimately afraid of Bruker House.

"I'm sorry, I didn't know," David said.

Charlotte put her hand on Alaina's shoulder. "It'll be okay, cher. You don't have Picatrix with you, but we'll all be together. You won't be alone."

Alaina took in a breath and sighed. She gently removed Charlotte's hand from her shoulder. "It's fine, what's done is done. Let's just go. We're all here now, aren't we?"

"We're still waiting on Hank, he's got the keys and knows the roads up to the house," David said. He pulled his phone from his pocket to check the time. "He should really be here any minute. I'd give him a call, but I'm not getting any signal up here."

"Speaking of heading up to the house... We're carpooling, right?" Charlotte asked. "The van only seats three, I was thinking I could ride with you, Ellie. It looks like you've got four-wheel drive in that thing, and I'd prefer to leave my little rental safe and sound on a paved surface."

"Yeah, you can ride with me. Are the roads up there really that bad?" Ellie asked.

"That's what they tell us," Lou said. "It's just a dirt road up to the house, and since it was abandoned, it hasn't been taken care of these last few decades."

"Not to mention the construction guys hauling stuff in and out all summer long," David said.

A white pickup pulled into the parking lot at a speed that said the driver wasn't very concerned with safety. Each axle crossed a dip at the lot's entrance and the cab rocked back and forth, testing the limits of the truck's suspension. A decal stamped across the side of the pickup read *Danver's Construction*.

"That must be him," David said.

The truck slowed to a stop near the group. A middle-aged man with a mustache and beard scruff leaned one elbow out the open truck window. He wore a blue chambray shirt and a green Dysart's trucker hat. "You folks the ghost hunters?" he asked.

David reached out a hand to shake. "You must be Hank. We have everyone here ready to head up when you are."

"Let's get a move on then. Follow me up the road and we'll turn off in a mile or so." Hank pulled his pickup to the edge of the parking lot, ready to lead the way.

"Just a minute, let me grab my bags," Charlotte said.

"What are you going to do with the car?" Ellie asked.

"Oh, it can stay here," Charlotte said. "Apparently the

restaurant owner is a big fan of the paranormal and wanted to help out with the investigation."

David turned back to the group. "Alaina, are you riding in the van with Lou and I or in the Jeep with Ellie and Charlotte?"

Alaina glanced at the Wagoneer, then to Ellie and Charlotte, and then down at Hux. Without a word, she picked her bag up off the ground and walked toward the van.

"I guess it's just you, me, and Hux!" Charlotte bent down to ruffle Hux's fur again. He let out an excited whine followed by a yawn.

"I think it'll take us about thirty minutes to get up to the house from here," David said. "Why don't I follow Hank, and you follow me? We'll drive real slow, but if anything happens and we get separated, just come back here. Don't try to find your way through those backroads on your own."

"Roger that," Charlotte said. She jumped into the Jeep's passenger seat and admired Hux in the rear. "He has such a cute face, I love his mask. It's too bad Alaina couldn't bring her cat too, I love meeting animals."

"Yeah, it's too bad," Ellie said somewhat dismissively while she followed David and Hank. "She said he was a familiar, didn't she? Like a witch would have?"

"Yeah, I can't say I'm surprised. Alaina seems a little witchy."

"I'm not quite sure if she really believes the things she says, or if it's all an act she puts on," Ellie said.

"I kind of know what you mean, but I think she's genuine. A lot of people feel a deep connection with their pets. They see them as a source of comfort or protection. Most people might call it an emotional support animal, but to Alaina, she calls it her familiar. In the end, I don't know if there's much difference. I think it's just two words for the same thing. Who knows, maybe Hux could be your familiar."

"I guess," Ellie said. She didn't agree with Charlotte that a familiar and an emotional support animal were the same, but she wasn't in the mood to argue.

They followed Hank into the hills for the better part of twenty minutes, the Wagoneer's cab swaying back and forth as the tires dipped into ruts and potholes. Finally, Ellie caught a glimpse of the house. It stood tall and imposing atop a hill, like a castle overlooking its domain. She had seen Bruker House in David's photos, but in person it somehow looked less real, like an illusion that had taken root in the wrong reality. It felt out of place, like it had been dropped into a spot where a house doesn't belong, an ornate Victorian mansion in the woods along the side of a muddy dirt road.

"I think that's it," Charlotte said. She leaned her head to the side of the cab and craned her neck to get a better look. "I think I see the gate up ahead too."

They drove a few hundred feet more when Hank stopped his truck in front of a large wrought-iron gate. It was flanked on either side by moss-covered stone walls stacked with enormous granite blocks. Ellie imagined the effort it must've taken to move the stone into the forest and up the hill. In her mind she pictured Egyptian slaves rolling massive stone blocks on logs to build the pyramids. A ridiculous image; Bruker House had been built well after mule carts and wagons made such feats manageable. Despite their formidable appearance, the walls were clearly meant for decoration, as they only extended fifty feet or so in either direction, after which someone could just walk around them onto the grounds. Ellie stopped the Wagoneer next to David's van and killed the engine. Her boots sank nearly an inch into the muddy road as she stepped out of the cab.

She tried to gauge her gut reaction and make a mental note of her first impression of the house. She thought maybe the hairs on the back of her neck would stand up, or a sudden chill would run down her spine; maybe a sickness would rumble in the pit of her stomach and cause her to vomit on the spot. Instead, all she felt was the cool damp air of the forest hills, the smell of pine pitch, and the sound of a light breeze as it passed between the trees. All she saw before her was a house. Wood, plaster, and glass. The house was old, isolated in a strange way, and in need of some repairs, but in the end that's all it was, just a house. Nothing more.

Hank stood in front of the gate. He reached into his jacket pocket and under the circumstances Ellie expected to see him pull out a comically large ring full of rusted skeleton keys and flick through them one by one until he found the key he was searching for. Despite the expectation set by decades of cartoons and Hollywood movies, Hank pulled out a normal modern-day key from his pocket and unlocked a mundane blue master lock. He unraveled the chain that secured the gate and pushed it open. The hinges groaned as metal rubbed against metal, and in response a bird called from the forest.

"Do you guys hear that?" Charlotte asked. "It's a whip-poorwill."

One by one the investigators crossed the threshold and

stepped onto the Bruker House grounds. The area beyond the gate was a barren courtyard. In its prime it may have boasted detailed landscaping and well-manicured gardens, but now tire tracks and deep ruts crisscrossed in the mud. Contractor trucks and construction equipment had ravaged any meager patches of grass that attempted to take root.

At the end of the courtyard stood Bruker House itself. The tall ornate Victorian stood in stark contrast against the forest, oddly misplaced this far from civilization. It would have been right at home in the center of an industrial-boom town, nestled between the decadent mansions of local business owners on a street named Broadway or High. A vestige of the days when it was fashionable to flaunt your wealth by building your home along the busiest street in town. The imposing facade of the house was crowned with a mansard roof and featured a central tower upright and proud at the home's front. Steps led from the courtyard onto a large porch adorned with ornate woodwork, and a set of double doors guarded the front entrance. The exterior of the house was painted blue-grey with a cream trim, and to Ellie the paint looked fresh. The only visible damage was a partially caved-in wing, which was more than Ellie could say for the carriage house next door, which still stood only by some miracle of gravity.

"There she is," Hank said. He flipped through several keys on his key ring as he walked toward the house. "All things considered, the house was in pretty good condition when we started work over the summer. We removed some overgrowth and repainted, but we've finished the exterior now and we're about halfway finished with the inside too."

"What about that other building back there?" Lou asked.

"The carriage house? Warwick wanted us to save it, but I think it needs to be demoed. I would advise you all not to go in there, the thing is about ready to collapse," Hank said.

"What about that one wing with the roof? Is it safe?" Ellie asked.

Hank didn't answer while he flipped through a few more keys on his ring, then he absent-mindedly said, "It's just the carriage house I'd worry about; rest of the house is safe."

The investigators followed Hank up the front steps onto the porch. He finally managed to find the key he was searching for—again, it was a standard modern-day house key and not the rusted old skeleton key that felt so appropriate. Hank unlocked the deadbolt and pushed the double doors of Bruker House open. There was no eerie creak, no swarm of bats flew out, no demonic screeching or disembodied voices commanding them to "Get out!" Beyond the doors lay nothing but a dimly lit old house.

Unlike the front door key, the entrance hall of Bruker House did live up to Ellie's expectation. It was two stories tall with a wide staircase rising along the left-hand side. A curve at the bottom of the stairs spilled out into the open space. An enormous glass chandelier hung from the second-story ceiling and dangled above an ornate red and gold rug and a beautiful wood floor inlaid with decorative patterns along each edge. On the second story, a landing wrapped around the perimeter of the entire hall and overlooked the foyer below. The home smelled of old wood and must, but with a subtle sour undertone.

"Wow," Charlotte said as she wandered into the center of

the hall and gazed up at the chandelier. "I guess the Brukers weren't hurting for money."

"They don't make 'em like this anymore," Hank said.

"If I could live in a place like this, I might even be willing to share it with a few ghosts," David said.

Hank looked at his watch. "I can give you a quick tour, but after that I gotta roll."

"That'd be great if you don't mind," David said.

Hank led the group into the parlor and Ellie noticed Hux wasn't with her. He was still outside in courtyard, staring at her through the double doors.

"What are you doing out there, silly boy?" Ellie asked.

He stared at her for a moment, then ducked his head down and picked a comically large stick up off the ground. He held it in his mouth and wagged his tail slowly.

"Not now, buddy, come on inside." Ellie waved him in.

Lou noticed the interaction between Ellie and Hux. "He doesn't want to come in. Maybe he senses something in the house."

Ellie scoffed at the comment. "Don't be silly, he just wants me to throw that stick. He's been cooped up in the car all day. Hux, come on!"

Hux dropped the stick and ran up the steps and through the front doors of Bruker House. "You need to stay with me, buddy!" Ellie said as she shut the doors behind him.

"The dog's smart. Whatever lurks in this house is probably safer than what's in those woods. You never know what you might find among the trees." Lou gazed out the front windows into the forest, not searching for a hidden threat among the oaks and maples, but watching a dark vision play out behind his eyes.

Hank led the team through a brief tour of the house. By Ellie's standards, Bruker House qualified as a mansion; others may call it a large house. The first floor had a kitchen, a parlor, a library, a dining room, a study, and of course a large entrance hall. The entire first floor, save for the study, had renovations in progress or complete, and was at least partially furnished. The second floor boasted nine bedrooms and three full bathrooms all connected by a long U-shaped hallway. Hank pointed out the exceedingly ugly yellow wallpaper in one of the rooms, and explained Mr. Warwick wanted to keep as much of the house original as possible. In fact, the only room of the house that had been significantly changed was the kitchen, now outfitted with modern commercial fixtures and appliances.

"You lucked out. Trust me, you don't want to eat takeout from any of the places in Narramissic," Hank joked.

The tour ended back where it began, in Bruker House's grand entrance hall.

"You can hang onto the key while you're here, I got a spare at the office anyway." Hank removed the front door key from his ring and handed it to David. "I'm going to leave the front gate and the swing gate at the bottom of the hill unlocked while you folks are here in case you need to leave."

"I appreciate that," David said. He stowed the house key safely in his front pocket.

Hank looked up at the ceiling while he counted out tasks on his fingers. "The kitchen has been stocked with all the basics for you, we did a tour, keys, what else? I assume you all can sort out the guest rooms on your own?"

"We can." David nodded.

"Oh! Cell service is spotty, as I'm sure you can imagine. You'll probably need to drive down to the bottom of the hill before you get a signal."

Alaina pulled her phone out of her pocket and scowled.

Ellie checked her own, the status in the corner confirmed *No Service*.

"I didn't even get good service back in Narramissic," Charlotte said.

"You all will survive a few days. Trust me, we got by just fine before those things came around." Lou gestured at the phones in each of their hands.

"Thanks for all your help, Hank. I'm sure we can take it from here," David said.

Hank took one more look at the group and gave a nod. "All righty then, I'll be back here Thursday morning to get the key from you and lock up. Until then, enjoy your stay. With any luck you'll be the first of many." The investigators thanked Hank and bid him farewell as he left through the large double doors. Ellie heard the engine of his pickup roar to life then grow faint as he drove back down the long and treacherous road to Narramissic.

Charlotte broke the silence. "This place feels so lonely. Can you image living out here, alone in this massive house in the middle of nowhere? I'm surprised more of the owners didn't go stir-crazy being cooped up in here."

"Don't speak too soon," Ellie said. "Maybe they did go crazy. After all, eleven people disappeared here."

"Good point," Charlotte said.

"Alaina, we've been in the house for a little while now, what are your first impressions? Have you felt anything yet?" David asked.

Alaina closed her eyes, took in a deep breath, and paused for a moment. "It's very faint, but yes, I do feel a presence here. It's distant though, dormant, buried almost."

"Does it feel aggressive? Demonic?" Lou asked.

Alaina stood in silence and breathed. Then, eyes still shut, she answered, "It feels dark, and cold."

Ellie rolled her eyes as she watched the dog and pony show play out. No psychic ever entered a haunted house and said they sensed a friendly spirit. *I'm sensing a name, it starts with a C. Did anyone in the audience lose a...a Casper?* Ellie thought. She glanced at Charlotte to gauge if they might be thinking the same thing, but Charlotte looked very invested in what Alaina had to say. So, Ellie kept the derision to herself.

David nodded. "Thank you, Alaina. Let us know if you pick up on anything else." He turned to address the rest of the group. "We should start setting up right away, there's only a few hours left until dark. Lou, can you help me unload the equipment from the van?"

"Yes, of course," Lou said. "I was thinking though, before we get started maybe it'd be good if we all say a prayer." He held out both of his arms waist high, palms forward, beckoning the others to join him.

"Sure we can, I think that'd be a great idea." David took Lou's right hand in his.

Charlotte, without uttering a word, took Lou's left hand.

"I'll pass," said Alaina.

All eyes turned toward Ellie, and Charlotte lifted a hand for her to join the prayer circle.

"I think I'll pass too," Ellie said.

David and Charlotte locked hands and closed the prayer triangle. Lou began with, "Dear Lord," followed by requests to bless the house and to keep the group safe during their stay. As the three of them affirmed their faith in the Lord, Ellie met Alaina's glance and was surprised by the quiet solidarity she felt. They may have disagreed on the supernatural, but they were at least on the same page when it came to prayer.

The prayer finished with an "Amen" spoken in unison, then David addressed the group again. "Charlotte and Ellie, we have six mountable cameras. I saw about a hundred good spots for them during Hank's tour. Why don't you go around and pick the spots that can cover the most ground?"

"Sure thing, Ellie and I will take care of it," Charlotte said.

"Great, and pick out a room to set up the monitoring station in while you're at it. Maybe one of the unfinished bedrooms? Lou, let's pull the van up to the house and start unloading."

Lou and David left to unload the van. Alaina sat down cross-legged in the center of the entrance hall floor to meditate. She picked a spot in the center of the luxurious oriental rug, directly beneath the elegant glass chandelier. Its tip pointed at her like a lightning rod.

CHAPTER 6

Ellie, Charlotte, and Hux walked together up the grand staircase to the second floor. "Isn't this house insane? I feel like I might turn a corner and bump into Colonel Mustard," Charlotte said.

Ellie laughed. "Yeah, I think I saw him in the library with the candlestick. It's bigger than any house I've ever lived in, that's for sure."

"Are you from Brookhaven originally?" Charlotte asked.

"No, I'm from Missouri. A small town called Fredrick's Bluff. Don't worry if you haven't heard of it, no one has," Ellie said.

"Oh, a Southern girl like me! Is your family all still back there?"

"Yes, but I'm not really close with any of them other than my aunt who raised me. Both of my parents have passed, not that I was close with them either." They reached the top of the staircase and took a left up the hallway toward the unren-

67

ovated bedrooms. Ellie prayed there wouldn't be any deeper questions about family along the way.

"I'm sorry to hear that, we don't have to talk about it," Charlotte said, picking up on Ellie's avoidance.

"What about you, where are you from?" Ellie asked.

"I've lived in Louisiana all my life. I grew up in Lafayette, then spent some time in Baton Rouge during college, New Orleans for a little while. Now I'm back in Lafayette again. Some people might think it's boring to live in the place you grew up, like you're going backward somehow, but for me, I wouldn't want it any other way."

"I don't think it's boring. Sometimes I wish I had a place that felt like home, but I couldn't wait to leave Missouri."

"I used to feel the same way. When I was a kid, I couldn't wait to get out of that town. Everything bad that had ever happened to me happened there, and in a way, I think I wanted to escape Lafayette to escape all that trauma. I wanted to live in the big city, to travel the world. I dreamt of spending years abroad in Paris, and having close-knit friend groups and passionate lovers from every continent. Then, as I got older, I found myself dreaming about Lafayette, that dumpy little town that I couldn't wait to leave. As time marched on, all those painful memories faded, all that trauma that consumed me for so long didn't seem to matter so much anymore. Eventually I admitted to myself that it was time to come home, and so I did." Charlotte placed a hand on the doorknob to the first unrenovated bedroom.

"I'm glad you found your way back home," Ellie said.

"Thank you. I've found my way back there in more ways than one. I think it's one of the most important things we can do in each life, to find our way home. It doesn't have to mean we go back to the place we're from, but we have to find who we are." Charlotte twisted the doorknob and pushed the bedroom door open. A few rolls of carpet and some drywall panels were propped against one wall, but otherwise the room had been stripped bare. "I vote we set up the monitoring station in here, and we can put a camera down that way overlooking the foyer and stairwell."

"This is my first rodeo, so I'll follow your lead," Ellie said.

Charlotte looked down at Hux. "How about you? Do you agree?" Hux responded with a blank stare and the smallest of tail wags. "He's a smart dog, I think he agrees. Probably just the one camera up here since we'll be sleeping in the bedrooms, but maybe we should take a look at the attic before we move downstairs."

The doorway to the attic was at the very end of the upstairs hallway. The door opened with a long, slow whine followed by several distinctive staccato pops as the hinges complained. Inside the door was the most unusual staircase Ellie had seen. Unlike a normal staircase, where one step spanned the entire width of the stairwell, each step only spanned half of the full width and alternated back and forth. It was as if each step were designed for just one foot at a time.

Charlotte let out a gasp as the door opened. "Witches stairs! You hardly ever see these anymore."

"Witches stairs? I've never heard of that."

"You see them in old houses in New England sometimes. Supposedly they were designed that way so witches couldn't walk down them. I guess it was to confuse them or something," Charlotte said.

"Was witches coming in through the attic a big problem back in the day?"

"Well, not in Bruker House it wasn't, because they had the super cool witches stairs to stop them. Come on, let's go up!"

Part way up the steps, Ellie heard Hux whimpering from behind them. He sat at the bottom of the stairs.

"Poor guy, he doesn't like the steps. Guess they're good for both witches and dogs," Charlotte said.

"We'll be right back, buddy," Ellie said to Hux. She continued up the stairs behind Charlotte.

At the top of the steep narrow staircase was a single large open space. The attic was empty save for a brick chimney stack on either side.

"Dark up here," Ellie said.

"Yeah, and I don't see any light switches."

"Should we put a camera up here?"

"Are you kidding me? This place is begging for one. Let's head back down, it's cold up here," Charlotte said.

By the time they made it back down to the entrance hall, David and Lou had unloaded several large black pelican cases and staged them in the foyer. Alaina was still sitting cross-legged in the center of the room, eyes closed, her breath slow and steady.

"We'll put a camera in the parlor and the library for sure. Let's take a look at the cellar," Charlotte said.

The staircase descending into the cellar had seen better days. The steps were made from bare unfinished wood, and without risers the space behind each step was exposed. "You know, when I was a kid, I was always afraid something would be hiding behind stairs like these, and they would grab my feet as I went down," Ellie told Charlotte as they descended into the cellar.

"Only as a kid?" Charlotte asked. "I'm still afraid of that now! We're literally in a haunted house, for Christ's sake!"

Bruker House was old, and like most old homes, the cellar was never intended to be used as livable space. It smelled of sawdust and damp earth. The cellar floor was dirt, and the walls were a mixture of stacked stone and bare wood. The few lonely bulbs scattered across the joists struggled to light the space. The cellar was divided into several separate rooms, most of them were filled with tools, equipment, and other building supplies, ready to be used again once the investigation was complete. Some rooms were used to store spare furniture or were stacked floor to ceiling with boxes of old personal belongings.

"Will you look at this mess, I think the previous owners may have been hoarders." Charlotte blew the dust off of a stack of yellowed magazines. "These things are from the thirties. *Collier's*? Never heard of it." She flipped through the top magazine, two smiling figure skaters posed on the cover.

Ellie dug through a stack of old newspapers. "Maybe of some of this stuff could be useful; there must be hundreds of these down here."

"Useful for starting a fire maybe. Half of these things are covered in mold, and the other half have dissolved back into pulp already."

Ellie opened an edition of *The Augusta Recorder* dated June 19, 1926. The sweet woody smell of old paper poured from the pages. The headline celebrated the winner of the annual Miss Damariscotta Pageant, a smiling young woman with short curls posed with a bouquet.

"Ellie, come over here, check this out," Charlotte said. She pointed at a dark space on the far edge of the cellar. Light from the underpowered bulbs barely touched it.

"What is it?" Ellie folded the newspaper and tossed it back atop the pile.

They walked across the cellar to the edge of the darkness. Charlotte pulled her phone out of her purse and turned on the flashlight. The small space was carved into the solid rock that Bruker House stood upon. Floors, walls, and even the ceiling were rough-hewn from stone. Water dripped from one corner and caused the stone of the floor to glisten with moisture. The ceiling height was lower than the rest of the cellar, five feet at most, and both Ellie and Charlotte had to crouch to see in.

"It looks like a cave," Charlotte said.

"It doesn't go back very far, maybe ten feet? I wonder if it's natural or if someone dug it out."

Hux sniffed at the edge of the small cave, and cautiously licked water from the wet rock of the floor.

"I wonder why someone would build it though. Wine cellar, maybe?" Charlotte asked.

Ellie shrugged.

"We should definitely set up a camera down here, maybe two, this place is creepy as hell. If we mount one back there by the staircase, we can get most of the cellar, even this here little cave."

"Will it be able to see in here?"

"The night vision on the cameras is pretty good. I think it'll work."

"All right, no argument from me. I'll admit, it is pretty creepy down here," Ellie said without much concern over camera placement.

By the time Ellie and Charlotte hiked back upstairs to the entrance hall, David and Lou had unloaded a total of six pelican cases, and David was already in the process of unpacking the first of them. Lou, breathing heavily, rested on an old sofa near the front door. Alaina hadn't moved an inch from her cross-legged pose.

David glanced at Ellie and Charlotte. "Perfect, we just brought in the last crate. Let's get set up and we'll be finished just in time for dinner."

Lou insisted on cooking for the five of them, six if you count Hux. He prepared an American staple, meatloaf with mashed potatoes and corn, and inspired by mid-century housewife tradition, the meatloaf was topped with Heinz ketchup in place of tomato sauce. The five guests sat down for their first dinner together around the long solid oak table of Bruker House's dining room. Floor-to-ceiling windows adorned one end of the room and framed the head of the table, which sat vacant. By rights, the chair belonged to David as the leader of the investigation, but he chose to sit two seats down from the head beside Ellie and Charlotte and across from Lou and Alaina. Ellie suspected that if Hux had been allowed to sit in a chair, he would gladly place himself at the head; instead, he nestled himself into a tight ball beside Ellie's feet.

"It feels like Thanksgiving," David said as he sat down.

Charlotte unfolded a napkin and gently placed it in her lap. "Thanks for cooking for everyone, Lou. It smells lovely."

"You're very welcome, young lady." Lou grunted as he set a large pan of meatloaf down beside a bowl that overflowed with mashed potatoes. "It's my wife's old recipe. She always said it doesn't count as real meatloaf unless you sauce it with ketchup."

"That's how my mom always used to make it too," David said.

Lou sat and looked around the table. "I was thinking, if it ain't too much ask, we could all say grace together before we eat. I know for some of you it isn't really your thing, but it'd make a real difference for me."

Ellie caught Alaina's eye. They knew exactly to whom Lou was referring. Charlotte, David, and Lou joined hands, and Lou gave another familiar prayer to the Christian god. While Lou gave thanks for the food, Ellie gave thanks that the prayer was short.

"Do you always pray before a meal?" Charlotte asked as she helped herself to several healthy scoops of mashed potato.

"Ever since I was a boy. Between the sisters at St. Matthews and my old man, I hardly had a choice. Now I'm older, I'm glad they taught me the habit," Lou said. He took the serving spoon from Charlotte and built his own mashed potato mountain. "And I'll tell you one thing, I sure as heck won't forget to stay in the Lord's good graces as long as I'm in this house." He poured gravy over his entire plate, covering a slice of meatloaf and turning the potato mountain into a gravy volcano.

Alaina refused the meatloaf as it was passed to her, and gave a look of disdain at the pan. She took only corn and a small portion of potatoes without gravy.

"Now that we got the equipment set up, what's the over-under on how long it'll take to catch Casper with his pants down?" Charlotte asked before she shoveled a fork full of mashed potatoes into her mouth.

"Let's not tempt fate. If this place is anything like half of our investigations, then we'll be going home empty-handed," David said.

Alaina picked at the food on her plate. She made a small dent in the potatoes and moved the corn back and forth with her fork. While the rest of them ate away Ellie had yet to see Alaina take a single bite.

"What do you say, Ellie? Think we'll come home empty-handed?" Charlotte asked. She gave a knowing smirk to Ellie and took another bite of meatloaf, smiling as she chewed.

"You already know what I'll say. I've never seen a shred of evidence for the paranormal, and I doubt Bruker House will change that," Ellie said.

"That puts you in the minority around this table. We get evidence all the time. Isn't that right, David?" Lou said.

David wiped his face with a cloth napkin. "I wouldn't say all the time, but at a place with a reputation like Bruker House? I'm pretty certain we'll get something."

Lou spoke with a mouth full of half-chewed food. "Sure, we don't find stuff at every place we go to, but if you do this long enough, the supernatural is undeniable. There's mountains of evidence out there, but the scientists, and the skeptics, and the atheists, they just refuse to acknowledge any of it."

Ellie set down her fork, ready for the first of what she assumed would be many arguments during her stay at the house. "How can you say that though? We've had cameras for well over a hundred years. Hell, most of us have carried one around in our pocket everywhere we go for the last twenty. There should be pictures of ghosts, and aliens, and Elvis all over the place. It should be such a routine occurrence that it's boring. Instead? Nothing. Which is exactly what you'd expect from something that didn't exist."

"I wouldn't say it should be routine though. There are plenty of things that are rare but are still real," Charlotte said.

"Sure, but there should be some pictures at least," Ellie said.

David finished eating and pushed his plate away. He leaned forward around Charlotte to speak directly at Ellie. His speech was calm, and he spoke to her in a tone reminiscent of her professor colleagues at Taconic. "There *are* pictures of ghosts though. You can search online and find dozens, if not hundreds of documented examples."

Ellie scoffed. She crossed her arms and leaned back in her seat. "I mean *real* pictures."

"They are real pictures," Lou said with a mouth half-full of food.

"You can't ask for pictures and then when you're shown them just write them off as fraud. That's called moving the goalpost," David said.

"I don't dismiss them off hand, but the only pictures I've

seen are clearly faked. Even if there are genuine photos out there, that's only enough to prove there's something we can't explain. You need positive evidence that something is, in fact, paranormal, not just a mystery. Plus, there's never been any corroborating evidence. Every paranormal claim out there is based on the word of just one or two people, and that makes it easy to stage a hoax. You never see large groups of people observing these things." Ellie struggled to hide the defensive tone in her voice.

"That last part isn't true actually," Charlotte said while setting down her fork. She, too, had finished eating and moved her plate away. The only person at the table still picking at their food was Alaina, who was eating in only the loosest sense of the word. "There are a few paranormal events that have been witnessed by large numbers of people. There was that thing that happened in Portugal. A crowd of people saw the sun swirl around in the sky."

Ellie shook her head. "I don't know anything about that."

Charlotte turned to Lou and then to David. "You guys know what I'm talking about, right? The sun thing in Portugal?"

David chimed in. "What Charlotte is referring to is called the Miracle of the Sun. It happened in Fátima, Portugal, in the early twentieth century. I want to say it was 1917? More than 10,000 people were there, they saw the sun dance around the sky and careen toward the Earth. It's well documented in newspaper reports, and there are even pictures."

Ellie knew going into it that she would have to respond to absurd claims, but until now she had underestimated just how far from reality they would stray. "That's absolute insanity, and I don't even know where to begin with it. The sun is millions of miles away and thousands of times larger than the Earth. It sure as hell didn't dance around in the sky. It's physically impossible! It's patently absurd to even suggest it!"

"All I'm saying is first you wanted photos, and we said there are photos. Then you wanted multiple eyewitnesses, and we showed you multiple eyewitnesses. Now I'm not sure what you want," Charlotte said.

"Sure, multiple witnesses suffering from mass hysteria maybe," Ellie said. She spoke slowly as if speaking to a child, and the defensiveness in her tone had shifted into frustration. "The claims need to make physical sense, they need to comport with reality as we know it."

"Reality as *you* know it," Lou said.

"Reality as it is!" Ellie said, a little louder than she intended.

Charlotte placed a gentle hand on Ellie's arm. "Hey, we aren't trying to gang up on you, but maybe these things do make physical sense, and we just can't prove it yet. There's plenty of things in science that don't seem to make sense at first, but we still know they're true."

"If that's the case, then the time to believe it is when we have evidence for it and not one moment before." Ellie tapped a finger against the table as she spoke to add emphasis to her point.

Alaina stopped picking at her food and set her fork down gently. In a voice barely above a whisper, she said, "And the time to believe there are lions in the lion's den is when you can feel their teeth against your skin."

"And you'll be the first to know when I get bit!" Ellie shot back.

The five of them were quiet, and Ellie wondered if she had taken things too far.

Alaina stood and picked up her uneaten plate. "I've been very tired since we arrived, I'm going to get some rest." She left the dining room through a heavy oak door that led into the kitchen. The door slammed shut and spoke louder than Alaina's words.

"I understand where you're coming from, Ellie. I really do," David said. "I don't think any of us here really think the sun swirled around the sky back in nineteen whenever, but I do believe that those people *saw* the sun swirl around, if you know what I mean. Exactly what they saw, I can't say, but to me, listening to them and hearing their story matters more than the math and science around planetary bodies. I think that lived experience is valid even if it can't be measured, or calculated, or verified by a panel of experts."

Ellie took a deep breath and grounded herself. She ran a hand across Hux's head, her fingers sinking deep into his fur. "I understand, but to me, personal experience just doesn't cut it."

"I expect nothing less from our skeptic." David leaned back deep into his seat and slapped both hands against his stomach. "Lou, you sure know how to make a meal. I'm tempted to follow Alaina off to bed, but someone needs to watch the cameras tonight. We can talk about shifts in the morning; I'll take the first night myself."

"The full night? Let me take half so you can get some sleep too," Charlotte said.

"No no, I'm always restless in new places. I'll do the full night and then be tired enough to sleep easy in the morning." David left the dining room and headed upstairs for the monitoring station. He was followed shortly after by Lou, who shuffled slowly to his guest room. Charlotte and Ellie cleared the table quickly, and wordlessly, before parting ways to their separate rooms.

Ellie shut the large wooden door to her bedroom; the old latch made a heavy clunk as it shut. She twisted a skeleton key in the old brass mortise lock and felt a satisfying resistance as the key pushed the bolt into place.

The Bruker House bedroom was just as ornate as the rest of the home. The centerpiece of the room was a king-size four-post bed that, to Ellie, looked like something Ebenezer Scrooge might wake up in while prattling on about ghosts. Atop the mattress was a luxurious comforter, large fluffy pillows, and high thread-count sheets. Hux jumped onto the four-poster and walked in a small circle twice before he settled down into a comfortable curl.

"Oh, you think you automatically get to sleep on the bed?" Ellie asked. She was answered by a deep sigh from Hux, who was exhausted from a hard day of doing nothing of consequence.

Ellie walked to one of the large picture windows to close the drapes. A waxing gibbous moon peeked between heavy clouds and bathed the forest below in silent silver light. Between the trees, in contrast with the moonlight, was a small yellow glow pulsing slowly, as if breathing. It was close, just beyond the tree line, less than two hundred feet from the house by Ellie's estimate. She wondered if it was an outbuilding, and made a mental note to explore the spot come morning.

She crawled beneath the covers of the large bed and tried to keep her mind away from the dinner table conversation. She unlocked her phone. No service. She wanted to message Ben and tell him about her first day, she was sure he'd get a kick out of it. She wanted to read the news, or mindlessly scroll through the internet. She wanted to reach something, anything beyond this isolated hill in Maine. Anything but to reflect on the truth: that she regretted her outburst at dinner, that she was embarrassed by it.

As she lay in bed with Hux, she was reminded of Thomas Huxley's words, *Sit down before fact like a little child, and be prepared to give up every preconceived notion without distraction.* Ellie decided she would commit to try harder to get along with the other four, regardless of their wild opinions. She would remain calm and try to understand their point of view.

She collapsed into the cool pillow and shut her eyes. Her stomach dropped at the creak of an opening door, a long slow whine followed by several distinctive staccato pops. Her heart thumped in her chest as she sat up. Her bedroom door was still shut, locked, but Hux stared at it, ears perked.

"Hello?" she murmured in the darkness.

The amber glow beneath the bedroom door went black as a shadow crossed. Ellie struggled to keep her breath quiet and listened. More pops sounded from the hall, followed by a whine and the click of a door latching.

It's just one of the others using the bathroom, get a grip, she thought to herself. She laid her head back onto the pillow, but her eyes stayed wide. She listened for the creak of a floor-board or the whine of a door hinge. She watched the shadows cast along the wall, born in silver moonlight that spilled around the curtain's edge. The outline of a vanity or a hulking creature lying in wait? Bedposts or demonic horns? A spot in the corner that no light touched, dark as midnight; would it twist and grow to envelop the entire room, pulling her into its carrion black abyss? Her eyes landed on her key ring on the side table, and its pink rabbit's foot charm. She brushed her fingers across its surface and remembered what her Aunt Shirley used to tell her as a child: *There's nothing there in the dark that wasn't there when the lights were on.* Ellie beckoned Hux from the foot of the bed and pulled him close against her chest. She shut her eyes and drifted into her first dreams within the walls of Bruker House.

CHAPTER 7

Ellie jolted awake in a strange room decorated with foreign furniture. For the second time this week, she awoke in a puddle of cold sweat. Nightmares had come to collect their due, and last night's vision of her father's brutality was even more vivid and intense than the one she had at home in Brookhaven.

In her mind, she still heard her mother's scream. A visceral snap echoed again and again as her father held her mother's shattered wrist in one hand and a bloody shovel in the other. Ellie ran. She ran through the fields and into the forest as her father gave chase. She ran until she reached the neighbor's house, only it wasn't a little white farmhouse next door, it was Bruker House. Her father yelled curses and nonsensical words from behind as he gave chase through the forest. Ellie entered Bruker House and slammed the door shut behind her. In her dream, the front door led directly into the cellar. She scrambled to find a place to hide. Her father kicked in the door and stared directly at her, infinite darkness burning behind his eyes. Through walls and stone and time itself he stared at her, stared through her. "I see you, Ellie. I see all of you," he said. He walked forward and dragged the shovel along the floor beside him. It left a sticky red trail of blood and brains in its wake. Ellie could feel vibrations in her teeth as the shovel's edge scraped against the floor. "They all died screaming," her father said as he lifted the shovel into both hands. "You'll die screaming too."

A familiar face popped up from the foot of the bed. Hux stretched and left his place to join Ellie by the headboard. She wrapped her arms around him, and he buried his muzzle into her chest. As she felt his warmth against her body, the visions of her father, the shovel, and the bizarre illogical version of Bruker House all faded away. They sunk into a small place in the back of her mind where dreams went to be forgotten.

Ellie peeled back the thick duvet and tried to ignore the unpleasant touch of sweat-soaked clothes against her body. She swung her feet off the bed onto the cold wooden floor and made a mental note to let Hank know the guest rooms needed area rugs. She worked the kinks out of her neck as she walked to the window and pulled back the heavy drapes to reveal the world beyond Bruker House. A deep orange sun sat low in the sky just above the horizon. Light mist covered the meadow behind the house and partially obscured the trees beyond. In the daylight she saw that the view across the grounds and to the distant hills and forest was spectacular. She looked between the trees for the place she had seen a glowing light the night before, but the morning mist was too heavy to make out any detail.

DAVID AND CHARLOTTE were sitting the dining room. Both of them were digging into plates loaded with scrambled eggs and toast.

"Lou made a big batch of eggs this morning before he took over the monitors. There's plenty left if you want some," Charlotte said between bites.

In the kitchen, Ellie poured a bowl of kibble for Hux and helped herself to the large pan of scrambled eggs on the stove. She joined the others at the dining room table.

"See any ghosts last night?" Ellie asked David as she sat down across from him.

"Cameras didn't catch a damn thing," said David. "But if I'm being honest, I might start to see things myself if I don't get some rest soon."

"They're probably saving their big debut for you." Charlotte nudged Ellie and smiled.

"I should only be so lucky," Ellie said.

"Well, I don't know if I'd call it lucky," David said as he took a sip of orange juice.

"What, seeing a ghost? Isn't that what we're trying to do here?" Ellie asked. She looked back and forth between Charlotte and David.

"Yes, but seeing one isn't necessarily a good thing. You could end up like Chrissy Taylor. She joined our investigations a few years ago. All she wanted in the world was to see a ghost, a full-bodied apparition. Sometimes I swear it was all she talked about. She would sign up for every investigation we did and always wanted to be right in the thick of it all. I'll be honest, I was more than happy to have someone with her enthusiasm on board, she did an enormous amount of work. Anyway, she joins maybe two dozen investigations, and after a couple years of doing it she finally got what she wanted. She saw a fully formed apparition with her own eyes. Of course, after that, not only did she never join another investigation, but the experience haunted her for years afterward. Last I heard she was still seeing a therapist every week and had to take sleeping pills every night to get any rest."

Charlotte set down her fork and shook her head. "If I knew you were going to bring that up, I would've left the room. I can't eat while thinking about that story with the faceless boy. It's like I can't get the image out of my head. I didn't even see it and it haunts me."

Ellie lifted her eyebrows and flashed a glance between Charlotte and David. "The faceless boy? What's that? What happened?"

David interlaced his fingers and leaned forward with his elbows on the table. "This was about seven or eight years ago. We were investigating the Cochrane family home out in Brockton. The woodshop murders. Have you heard of them? It would've been in the late nineties."

Ellie thought for a moment but didn't recall the name. She shook her head.

Charlotte's face distorted in disgust. "I can't listen to you tell it, I'm sorry. I'm done eating. I have a half-dozen trail cams I need to set up this morning anyway." She collected what was left of her breakfast and wiggled a fork at Ellie. "You might want to finish eating that before you hear any more of the story." After she left the room, she popped her head back in again. "On second thought, you might not want to hear any more of the story at all."

"She's right, you know. The murders were a bit... gruesome. Are you sure you want me to tell it?" David asked.

Ellie nodded and swallowed a mouthful of coffee. "Yes, I think I can handle it."

David took in a deep breath. "Okay. You've been warned. The faceless boy is a nickname for one of the spirits at the Cochrane house. As you probably guessed already, he was a victim of the woodshop murders: Billy Cochrane, the youngest of the four children. He was murdered along with the rest of the family by his father Joseph. All of them were killed brutally, but I think most people would say Billy got it the worst."

Ellie took another bite of her eggs and worried that it might be the last she would want.

"On the night of the murders, Joe Cochrane woke up his wife and kids one by one and led them out back into the woodshop. He was a carpenter, you see, and the house had this huge shop out back full of every tool you can imagine. By the time he led Billy into the shop, he had already murdered his wife and two of his other children in...creative ways. I don't know what possessed Joe to do the things he did, but he killed each one of them with a different tool, and for Billy it was the bench sander."

Ellie regretted that last bite of egg. She had a sinking feeling that she might be seeing it again very soon.

"I don't know how long he held that boy's face against the sander, but I saw the crime scene photos while I was doing research for the investigation. Let me just say, those images stick with you. There was nothing recognizable left of little Billy's face. He looked like an abstract painting, just a mess of blood and bone. What's worse is according to the coroner's report, it wasn't the trauma from the sander that killed him. He died asphyxiating on his own blood. God knows how long that boy suffered."

David stared out the large dining room window and took a few sips of orange juice. He spoke slower when he continued. "The family reached out to us for an investigation after several people claimed to have seen Billy in the house, what was left of him anyway. Of course, Chrissy signed up for the investigation just like she signed up for damn near every one we did back in those days. She got up during the night to use the bathroom, and while she was on the toilet she saw a shape in the corner of the room, just a silhouette, but there was something in there with her. She flicked on the bathroom light and this young boy was standing in the corner staring at her, his face a bloody mess of flesh and empty gaping holes where the eyes and mouth should have been. She said her heart stopped beating right then and there; it didn't start up again until several minutes later when she was finally able to scream. As for the rest of us, we just heard the screaming and, of course, by the time we made it to the bathroom, the apparition had faded. Poor Chrissy was there on the floor, half-dressed, screaming and rambling. It must've taken us a full hour to calm her down again. That was the last investigation Chrissy ever went on. I only spoke with her a few times after that, and she said she had nightmares about the faceless boy every night. She said sometimes she would wake up screaming; other times she couldn't get to sleep because she was paranoid that the boy was staring at her from every shadow."

"I assume you didn't have any cameras set up in the bathroom?" Ellie asked.

David chuckled. "No, I don't think that would've gone over very well with the crew."

"That's too bad, but I can't say I blame them."

"Anyway, I guess all I'm saying is, be careful what you wish for. Chrissy thought she wanted to see an apparition, but it terrified her enough to affect her life for years to come. For some people it's traumatic to witness a paranormal event like that. It could change you."

Ellie nodded her head. "I don't disagree. Seeing a ghost would certainly turn my world upside down."

The two sat in silence for a moment before David stood up from the table and cleared his plate. "I really need to get some shut-eye, or I won't be able to function much longer."

"I need to get started for the day too. I wanted to ask, is there anything you need from me this morning? I was planning on looking around the house and grounds on my own some today. Maybe doing a little investigation for any practical explanation for the disappearances here."

David shook his head. "No, we've got Lou on the monitors and Alaina was working on some EVPs. I think you can drive the non-paranormal side of the investigation however you'd like."

Ellie fed the eggs that remained on her plate to Hux, and prepared for her first full day at Bruker House.

THE MORNING WAS cold and heavy. What little sunlight managed to break through the clouds warmed the air to just above freezing, but a thin layer of frost remained in the shadows. On this hillside in Northern Maine, autumn was near its end, and winter had begun to stir.

Hux, always her shadow, followed Ellie out through the front doors and ran to collect the oversized stick he'd found when they first arrived. He gnawed on the end of it and growled, then flung it in the air to show off his prize. He stared at Ellie and wagged his tail slowly, daring her to throw it. Ellie obliged the request and threw the stick as far as she could into the woods. Hux sprinted at top speed, plowing through fallen leaves and branches, then bolted back to Ellie and dropped the stick at her feet for round two.

Ellie walked toward the collapsing carriage house. Its barn doors were long gone; in their place, a dark and gaping maw opened into a dusty and dilapidated interior. Light seeped through holes in the roof and walls. What little paint remained clung to each board in quiet desperation. Ellie considered entering the carriage house for a closer look, but the roof was partially collapsed, and it looked like nature was poised to finish the demolition at any moment. She decided her investigation would need to take place from the doorway, lest she become the twelfth missing person at Bruker House.

As it stood, there wasn't much inside the carriage house to investigate. A tractor was parked along one side, so old and rusted that its valves and gears had fused into a single hulk of metal long ago. Tools hung from the back wall. Ellie's eyes scanned over a massive crosscut saw blade built to be operated by two people, pitchforks and rakes, an axe, and even a bloody shovel. Her eyes darted back to the shovel as it leaned steadily against the wall. The rusted shovel was caked with dirt. No blood.

Ellie carried on past the carriage house in search of the light she'd seen the evening before. At the edge of the forest, she looked back at Bruker House to her bedroom window to ensure she was in the right spot. She found no other buildings, no light posts, nor any object to explain what she had seen. The woods were empty save for the trees and a thick blanket of leaves on the forest floor.

Hux dropped the stick at Ellie's feet and she threw it as hard as she could along the tree line. It spun end-over-end down the hill to the west end of the once grand but now forgotten Bruker House grounds. At the bottom of the hill, Charlotte was strapping a trail cam around the base of a large maple.

"Charlotte!" Ellie called out. She waved as she trudged down the hill to meet her.

Charlotte turned with a smile and gave an enthusiastic wave back. Hux collected his stick, but instead of returning it to Ellie, he ran toward Charlotte and deposited his prize at her feet. She granted his request, and hurled the stick into the grass.

"Setting up some trail cams?" Ellie gestured toward a small pelican case sitting open at the base of a tree. Several cameras were stacked inside, along with packs of batteries, several flashlights, and a large can of bear spray.

"I am. I really should've done it last night, but ran out of time before dark. I got three up on this side of the property, and I plan to set up two more over there on the east side." She waved vaguely into the woods as she spoke. "I figure if we want to have a chance of finding anything out here, I better get these bad boys covering as much area as possible."

Ellie reached into the pelican case and picked up one of the small cameras painted in hunter's camouflage. "You really think you'll catch Bigfoot on one of these things?"

Charlotte laughed. "Certainly not. I don't think anyone is serious about cryptids at Bruker House, but according to David, the guys who bought this place paid a pretty penny for the full suite of experts. So here I am."

"I guess he's supposed to be up in Washington anyway, huh? Bigfoot, I mean."

"That's what they say. Though there are other cryptids native to the northeast. Wendigos are probably the most famous of 'em." Charlotte pulled the strap tight on the camera she was mounting.

"Oh, I've heard of that one, it's like a man with a deer head."

"Well, not really." Charlotte finished adjusting the camera strap and wiped her hands. "The deer-man version is from a short story written by some old white dude. The original wendigo is an Algonquin legend. They're humans who've eaten the flesh of another human and turned into a vicious corpse-like monster. More like a vampire than a deer-man."

Ellie raised her eyebrows. "You really believe in all that?"

Charlotte smiled and pulled her knitted cap down a little farther over her ears. It was cold enough that Ellie could see her breath as she spoke. "I think it's possible there is truth mixed in with the legend. I don't know if people have ever really turned into monsters because of cannibalism, but I think the Algonquins knew this land and knew the things that roamed in it. I can't rule out that there is something out here that inspired the wendigo myth."

"If that's true, don't you think we'd have caught one by now?"

"No, not at all, actually. You see, animals don't want to be found, they put quite a lot of effort into hiding. We have a long, storied history of scoffing at the claims of native people when they tell us about their land. Just look at the okapi. It lives in a small remote part of the Congo. For decades, Europeans in Africa thought it was a myth; hell, even seeing one in zoo, the thing looks made-up, like something a child would draw. Turns out the okapi is as real as you and me. There's this bizarre hubris we seem to have, that man has some kind of domain over nature, that we know everything there is to know about her secrets, but nature don't belong to us and the animals that live in these wilds are under no obligation to announce their presence."

"I feel like I might've hit a nerve there."

"Not so much a nerve as it is something I spend a lot of time thinking about. Mother Nature has a right to her secrets, and I kind of like it that way. Plus, you never know what you might catch on these things." Charlotte took the camera from Ellie, turned it over in her hands, then tossed it back into the pelican case. "There's no rule that says ghosts can't wander around outside too, but more likely than not, we'll get some really nice footage of deer and racoons!"

Charlotte shut the pelican case lid. The latches that held

it shut made a satisfying chunky sound as she pushed them into place. "What are you doing out in this cold anyway?"

"Well, while everyone else investigates this place for ghosts and goblins, I figured I could do an investigation of my own. You know, try to solve Bruker House's non-paranormal mysteries." Ellie threw the stick for Hux for what felt like the hundredth time this morning; he would chase the thing all day long if she let him.

"I would've thought you'd say all of Bruker House's mysteries were non-paranormal?"

"They are, yes." Ellie smirked.

"Wouldn't that be a turn of events? We all get contracted to come up here to give this Warwick guy evidence of some ghosts, and you wind up explaining the whole damn thing without a hint of the paranormal. I'd love to see the look on his face after what he's paying for all this."

"I doubt I'll find anything that all the other searches missed, but I figured I should do my part as the only skeptic here. Plus, it's kind of silly I know, but when I was reading about the missing persons cases, I felt a connection with some of them. I just felt this compulsion to come," Ellie said. She thought about Julie Campbell, her bruised, lifeless eyes.

Charlotte's face changed from her usual bubbly and easy-going expression to one of seriousness and intrigue. "What you mean you felt compelled?"

"I don't know, just that it felt like it was the right thing to do."

Charlotte was silent as she picked up the pelican case, but behind her eyes was deep thought. "Want to walk back up toward the house with me? I still need to set up a few cameras on the other side, but I could use some company on the way."

"Sure." Ellie nodded. She and Hux walked with Charlotte along the tree line back toward the house, Ellie occasionally throwing a stick as they went.

"You know, it was strange for me to hear you say you felt compelled to come here. At first, I wasn't going to come myself. Maine is an awful long way to travel from Lafayette just for some house I'd never heard of, plus it's cold as shit up here, but then I had the damnedest feeling that something important was going to happen. Of course, I don't have a gift in the way Alaina does, but maybe we all have it some of the time, just a little bit, you know? Something in me said I was meant to come. Like I'm supposed to do something or have some kind of transformative experience here. Does that make any sense?"

"It sort of does, yeah."

"Between you and me, I don't think there are any cryptids here. These cameras are probably a waste of time. Warwick and his goons just thought having a cryptozoologist on the team sounded cool. As an expert, my being here is kind of useless, but I really do think this place will have a critical moment for me this time around. Hell, maybe for all of us," Charlotte said.

"This time around? You plan on coming back?"

"Oh, by this time around I mean in this life." Charlotte adjusted the case in her hand as she walked and shifted its weight to a more comfortable position. "I'm big into past lives, reincarnation and all that. I believe we've all lived countless lives before this one. Thousands of lives, maybe millions, in this world and in others. I think we find our lovers again and again, we cherish each other and grow. We find our adversaries, they challenge us, and we overcome them in a thousand lifetimes before this one and a thousand more after. Most importantly though, I think we find ourselves. Moments to discover who we truly are outside of these bodies and these short lives."

Ellie nodded in silence as she tried to wrap her head around Charlotte's worldview. "You're saying in this life there's something important you need to do here at Bruker House?"

"I don't know it for sure. I just have a feeling that there's something I need to do, or to see, or maybe even something I need to say to someone else. I believe most of what we do day-to-day in our lives is up to us to have fun and enjoy our time here. But there are a few pivotal moments and choices that we *need* to experience, and our actions in those moments are what determine where we go next. Almost like a test."

"What's a pivotal moment look like?"

"I've already had one in this life, a big one," Charlotte said. They were near the carriage house now and Charlotte stopped walking. She set the pelican case on the ground and turned to Ellie, her face painted with a serious expression. When she spoke, her voice was quiet and sincere. "I'm not sure if anyone told you, or if you may have figured it out on your own, but I was assigned male at birth. I didn't transition until college."

Ellie shook her head. "I had no idea."

"I believe that my choice to transition was *the* pivotal moment in this life." Charlotte looked out over the Bruker

House grounds and sat down on the pelican case lid. "You see, I think the part of me that lives on, my soul or essence or whatever you want to call it, the real me, is female. Always has been. I believe that in every other life I've lived I was assigned female, because, well...that's just who I am. In this life, though, I was given a challenge. I was born into a male body, and I had to make the choice whether to accept the wrong body and the wrong life, or to be true to myself, true to my soul. It wasn't easy, but in hindsight I made the only choice I could've lived with, to present as my true self. The choice went against social expectations, I lost friends and family, I took on the risk of bodily harm from people who would hate me just because of who I am." Charlotte paused on those last words and Ellie saw pain written on her face. Her lip trembled as she spoke again. "But despite all that, if I could do it all again, I would do it in a heartbeat. In this life and ten thousand more." Charlotte wiped the corner of her eyes and gazed out across the grounds into the cold misty morning.

Ellie sat down on the pelican case beside Charlotte and put her arm around her shoulder. "I think that's really beautiful, Charlotte. Thank you for sharing that part of your life with me."

Charlotte smiled and put her hand on top of Ellie's. "I know you don't believe any of this hippy dippy bullshit, and that's okay, because I think you're a good person and a good soul, and in the end that's all that really matters."

"I think you're a good person too, despite the hippy dippy bullshit," Ellie said. Both women laughed, and Charlotte wiped the corners of her eyes one last time.

Hux plopped the stick at Ellie's feet and nudged her knee, begging her to throw it. Ellie groaned and threw the stick into the trees. Hux bolted toward it, kicking up leaves in his wake.

"Hey, what is that?" Charlotte asked. She pointed to where the stick landed. There was a small gated-off area in the forest; within it was an obelisk surrounded by several smaller stones.

"It looks like a little cemetery, maybe a family plot?" said Ellie.

"Let's take a look."

Ellie counted nine headstones in total. The obelisk in the center read *BRUKER* in large block letters recessed deep into its granite face. The smaller stones which surrounded it belonged to various members of the Bruker family. Ellie recognized a few of the names from the documents collected by David. There was Mary Bruker, only three years old, whose body was never found, and whose grave Ellie presumed was empty. Beside her was Alexander, who had built the house. There was a Jonathan and a Virginia Bruker, and beside her a small stone inscribed with one short word that spoke so many more. *Baby*.

"Look at this one," Charlotte said. She stood in front of a headstone which read:

HELENA BRUKER

1838 – 1889

MAY SHE REST

Unlike the other six graves, this one had a large flat slab of granite at the foot of the headstone that extended across the plot itself.

"Why do you think this one gets the fancy stone above the grave?" Charlotte asked.

"It's Alexander's wife. Maybe he wanted to do something special for her."

"Or maybe he didn't want her getting out."

"Charlotte, Ellie!" David's voice cut through the forest, calling out from behind them. "If you guys are out there, come back to the house. Lou found something!"

CHAPTER 8

The five investigators huddled together in the makeshift monitoring station. The room felt large when Ellie saw it on her first day at Bruker House; it was empty then, save for a few construction materials stacked along the far wall. Today, the room was claustrophobic. The construction material was now joined by two chairs, several folding tables supporting a bank of computer monitors, and no less than six empty pelican cases scattered around the room. What little space remained was now occupied by five humans and a dog clustered around a single display screen.

David clicked through several tabs on the computer until he found the folder he was searching for. "It happened at 9:23, right?"

"On the dot! Start playing a little earlier though," Lou said.

David opened a video file. The title said it was captured from *Camera 3 – Parlor*. He dragged a slider in the video player to 9:22 and clicked play.

"All right, look closely," David said.

Ellie watched in anticipation as the timestamp in the corner of the screen clicked forward, her eyes darting back and forth between it and the video playback. Every second seemed to tick by at glacial speed. Just before 9:23, Lou broke the silence. "Here it comes, watch!" A moment later, a shadow moved across the parlor from the left side of the screen to right. It passed in no more than a second.

"Holy shit, what was that? Is there any more?" Charlotte asked.

"No, that's it," Lou said.

"Roll it back, I want to see it again," Charlotte said.

David dragged the slider back to a few seconds before the shadow crossed the room. Ellie watched carefully as it crossed the screen from left to right. She had to admit, whatever it was, it was unusual, but of course that didn't mean it was supernatural. David played the video again at quarter speed. The frames stuttered by, and in slow motion it looked as if a black snake slithered across the room from one side to the other. It entered from the left, overtook the entire screen for a few frames, and then slithered back out on the right.

"Would you look at that, and on our first day too! Nobody was in the room at the time?" Charlotte asked.

"No one was even downstairs," David said.

Charlotte and David high-fived and Ellie jumped at the crack. For a moment, she was running through the forest, her father screaming obscenities behind her. She closed her eyes and suppressed the vision.

"Looks like your standard shadow figure to me," Lou said.

"That was my take too," David said. "Make sure we back

up the file and note down the time in the log. Save the highest res version of it you can."

"Roger that," said Lou.

"Shadow figure?" Ellie asked.

"They're a common apparition. They aren't full-bodied, but they're kind of...part way there, if that makes sense," Charlotte said. "They can come in different forms. Humanoid is very common, especially a man wearing a brimmed hat like a fedora, but they can also just be a shadowy mass like this one."

"Has anyone been in the parlor since this spirit appeared?" Alaina asked quietly from the back of the group.

"I did take a look myself while David was searching for the rest of you. I didn't see anything unusual though," Lou said.

"I'll see if I can tap into anything," Alaina said. She vanished from the room in silence, as if she herself were a ghost.

"What's your take, Ellie?" David asked.

"I don't know. It's weird, I'll say that much, but not so weird I'd jump straight to calling it supernatural. There could easily be a physical explanation for something like this. A trick of the light, camera malfunction, something."

David nodded and plopped down into one of the wheelie chairs in front of the bank of monitors. "Well, if you come up with anything, let us know. I'll include every perspective in my report at the end of all this."

"You're sure no one was near the parlor at 9:23?" Ellie asked.

David shook his head. "No one. Unless there's a sixth

person in the house with us. I was asleep in my room, Alaina was in an empty bedroom collecting EVPs, and Lou was here in the monitoring station. You and Charlotte were both outside. Hux, too, for that matter."

"Any way it could be the camera, some kind of glitch or artifact?"

"No reason to think so. Camera six in the attic cut out a few times last night, but the camera in the parlor seems to be working just fine. Plus, I've been using this brand for years and I've never seen something quite like this before."

"Camera six was cutting out during the prison investigation last month too. You need to replace it," Lou said.

David sighed. "I know, I'll look into it once we get back to Brookhaven."

As much as Ellie wanted to blame the shadow on human error or equipment malfunction, there was no justification for it. As usual, the low-hanging fruit had been ruled out, and it would take a clever model to explain what the camera had captured.

"Let's see it one more time," Charlotte said. The excitement was barely contained in her voice.

David started the playback again, but Ellie wasn't interested in sticking around to watch the footage; she'd seen enough. Yes, a shadow had moved across the parlor, but shadows aren't supernatural. All she needed to do was explain what had caused it.

"I think I'll head down and take a look at the parlor along with Alaina," Ellie said.

Hux followed her every footstep as Ellie descended the broad staircase to the first floor. On their way down a small bell rang. Its sound was light and pleasant, like two champagne glasses toasting. Hux's ears perked and he trotted toward the parlor.

Alaina sat cross-legged on the floor in the center of an elegant Turkish rug. Today she had forgone the black-and-white movie star look in favor of a flowy dark green dress. In front of her was a small wooden trunk inlaid with black and gold geometric patterns. Several trinkets were scattered across the floor around her: candles of various colors and sizes, incense, dried sage and other herbs, an ornate metal bowl, an amethyst crystal, a set of scales, and a small brass bell that looked like it would be right at home in a Buddhist shrine. Ellie assumed it was the bell that had chimed as she and Hux made their way downstairs.

"Tap into anything yet?" Ellie asked.

Alaina turned and her face showed that she was unamused, annoyed at Ellie's disruption. "No, not in this room at least. I do sense something in the house as a whole though."

"How do you sense it? Can you explain it to me? I mean, to me this place is just a house. It's wood and glass and plaster and nothing more. What is it that you see that everyone else can't?" Ellie asked.

Alaina paused for a moment while holding a carved wooden figure in her hand. She looked down at it and brushed a finger along its length, then placed it back into the trunk. She turned around in her cross-legged position to face Ellie, and she spoke with a tone of quiet frustration. "I've been mocked and interrogated for my gift all my life. Skeptics like you call me a con artist, the religious call me a witch, doctors call me crazy. Sometimes even believers call me a liar when I tell them something they don't want to hear. I don't need to justify myself to you or to anybody. I have no interest in convincing you of anything at all. To be frank, I couldn't care less whether you believe or not." She turned back to her small chest and removed several small crystals.

Ellie sat in an old worn leather chair, and Hux jumped into the seat beside her. Since she arrived at Bruker House, Ellie had mostly avoided the supposed psychic. Of the four investigators, Alaina's worldview seemed to differ the most from her own, and Alaina hadn't exactly been subtle about her opinions. Now, seeing her on the floor with her box of trinkets, Ellie wondered if it might be time to make peace. If she was going to spend the next two days with her, she might as well push through and try to get to know the woman.

"I'm sorry if my questions came across that way. I'm not asking you to justify anything, I'm just curious what it's like for you. What your experience is like."

Alaina paused again and turned to look Ellie in the eye. At first her lips were pursed, but then they began to relax. She took a deep breath before she spoke. "It's not easy to explain to someone who doesn't have it. It's like explaining color to the blind, or music to the deaf. There just aren't words to describe it without a point of reference. I can give analogies, but that's the best I can do."

Alaina turned her eyes to the ceiling for a moment and then looked down at her lap and fiddled with her bracelet while she spoke. "People get impatient with me and others like me because we can't always give them exact answers, but our experience isn't like reading something out of a book or seeing it clearly in front of our faces. It's more like a sense of smell, or like tasting a bite of food and trying to name what spices were used to flavor it. Some flavors might be obvious and stand out, but so many others are subtle, or they interact with each other in complex and confusing ways."

Alaina looked up from her lap and panned her eyes across the parlor. "This house, for example, has layers upon layers of complexity, as so many old homes do. They're touched by the lives of so many people who live within their walls, so many emotions and words spoken over hundreds of years, they flow like ripples across the decades, or sometimes like tidal waves. Most of the layers in Bruker House aren't very notable—the echo of a couple's rage after an argument, the fear felt by a small child alone for the first time, the cold shroud of grief after the loss of a loved one. Occasionally there's a layer of immense joy too, but for some reason the joy never seems to stick around quite as long as the pain. Here in Bruker House, though, there's something buried beneath it all. Something vile that leaves a metallic taste in your mouth. So revolting that it makes you want to puke and never sully your mouth with flavor again. It's deep and it's old, and it doesn't want to be found, but it's here."

Ellie nodded her head. Despite her conviction that no one really had psychic powers, and that such a thing didn't even make physical sense, Alaina did do a good job of explaining her experience. Ellie started to think that Alaina really did believe in her ability, that she thought what she was doing was real and important. "What about people? On your podcast you read people too, right? They have these complex layers?"

"Yes, of course. People usually have even deeper and more complex layers than any house ever could. Although I will say, the depth of Bruker House comes closer to that of a person than other place I've been to."

"What about me? Can you tell me what you sense in me?"

Alaina frowned in exasperation. "I don't do parlor tricks. Like I said, I'm not interested in being tested by you."

"Not a test. I'm genuinely curious what you sense in me."

A frustrated look on Alaina's face turned to an expression of sadness and pity. She looked in her lap again as she spoke, fixated on fiddling with her bracelet. "You carry a lot of pain. There are a few things that stand out right away—your loneliness, your pride, your fear, especially a fear of the unknown. Above all else, though, I sense childhood trauma. It was the first thing I saw in you when you walked into the room back in Brookhaven. That trauma is like a thousand-pound mass of putrid waste chained to your back, it drags you down with every step you take, the stink radiates from you and follows you wherever you go."

Ellie sat silent for a moment as she took in Alaina's words. She stroked the back of Hux's head as he sat beside her, her fingers disappearing into his fur. She nodded her head slowly. "I wish I could say you were wrong."

"You wouldn't be the first to tell me it was just a lucky guess, to say that I'm a talented fraud, but a fraud nonetheless. The thing is, though, I don't really care what you think. You asked what I sensed, and I told you."

"It isn't like that. I think you're very good at reading people and picking up on subtleties, and maybe you've fooled yourself into thinking its something more. I just don't believe in a sixth sense."

Alaina shrugged. "Don't care."

"Is it really that obvious? My childhood?"

"Like it's written on your forehead. Don't take it personally though. I see it all the time, and it doesn't say anything negative about you, only about how you've been treated by others. I'm all too familiar with it myself. I have my own thousand-pound pile of garbage to drag around with me. It's lighter now than it used to be, I've left as much of it as I can to rot away in the past. Maybe someday I'll be able to leave the rest of it behind too."

"I guess that makes two things we have in common then. Bad childhoods and opting out of group prayers."

The corners of Alaina's lips raised into the faintest of smiles. "Yes, but Yahweh does exist. I just don't participate in incantations that evoke a being as vile and full of rage and bloodlust as that one. There are many better and cleaner protection charms out there, and I prefer making requests to beings who don't demand a blood sacrifice."

"Well, there's a perspective I haven't heard before. Maybe don't mention that to Lou," Ellie said.

Alaina's smile grew and she snorted. It was the first laughter Ellie had heard since she met the woman. "Speaking of protection charms."

Alaina reached into her trunk with both hands and pulled out an object much larger than the rest of her trinkets. From the way she shifted her body to remove it from the trunk, it was clear that the object held some weight. It was wrapped in an ornate cloth woven from deep red and green fibers. She set it down carefully onto the rug in front of her and gently unwrapped the cloth to reveal a worn leather-bound book. There were no words on the spine that Ellie could see. The cover was embossed with a circle divided into six segments. Within each segment was a different symbol. To Ellie, they looked like a stylized sun, a triangle containing an eye, a five-pointed star, a crescent moon, a stylized *h* with a line across the top, and three intersecting swirls.

"What is it?" Ellie asked.

Alaina removed two silk gloves from the trunk and put them on before she touched the book. She opened the front cover as carefully as any person could, and gently turned the first few pages. "It has no official name or author; if it ever did, it's long lost to history. When my foster mother passed this book onto me, she called it *The Wheel*. She said it had been passed on to her by her mentor when she was young, and he refused to tell her where it came from. He told her when he received it that it had a name which he couldn't repeat, but even that wasn't its true name."

"That's...strange," Ellie said. Alaina turned more pages, and Ellie saw the book wasn't written in English, or even in Latin characters. "What language is that?"

"This is Enochian. Some of the other passages are in Latin, some in Greek, and a few others are in languages lost to time."

"So, it's a spell book? A book of magic?"

Alaina stopped turning the pages and landed on one which depicted a circle enveloped by several interlocking stars. Enochian symbols were scrawled around the circle's inner edge. "More like *the* book of magic. There are a lot of books out there that claim to be magic, and almost all of them are horseshit. A few widely available books do have some real spells, maybe five percent of *The Key of Solomon*, a few phrases in *The Corpus Hermeticum*, but really, they're just souvenirs. Real books of magic are rare, extremely rare. I've been practicing the crafts for nearly a decade now, and I only know of two other texts in existence with real power.

"*The Scourge of Belial* is kept deep in the library of the Basilica de San Salvador in Seville. There's an order of monks that guard the room it's kept in, but they aren't permitted to enter. It's kept under constant lock and key unless Vatican leaders request to view it. I have a friend who's like me—sensitive, I mean. She said she was on a train ten miles outside the city when she felt it. She said never before in her life had she felt something with that much power, that it was a deep and hateful power. Then there's the *Byblos Codex*, which is in Meg Sanderson's private collection in New York. I got to see it once. Meg even offered to let me read through the pages, but even being in the same room with it made me nauseous." Alaina stroked a few gloved fingers down the open page of *The Wheel* and looked up at Ellie. "Again, I don't care what you believe."

"I didn't say anything," Ellie said.

Alaina looked back down at the page in silence.

"If it's so rare, why bring it with you here and not keep it locked up at home?" Ellie asked.

"The text in *The Wheel* has power, *real* power. There are a lot of people out there who would like to get their hands on it. I don't let the book out of my sight."

Ellie was certain that Alaina believed every word of what

she said. Alaina was convinced this dusty old tome contained magic with the same conviction that a priest believed the Bible was the word of God. To Ellie, though, it was just another trinket. It was no more valuable than the books full of voodoo that could be found in any third-rate crystal shop. "And what about all this other stuff? The candles, the rocks, they seem like things anyone could buy."

"It may seem that way, but it's not. Have you ever heard of a cargo cult?"

Ellie was familiar with the term, but she had to dig deep in her memory to find it. She had read about them in an old Carl Sagan book. "Yes, Pacific Islanders who mimicked American soldiers after World War II. They built control towers out of bamboo and cleared airstrips. They marched around every morning like the soldiers did in a sort of bizarre ritual."

"Well, the same thing happened with the crafts. People saw clairvoyants use objects of power." Alaina placed her gloved hand onto the open pages of *The Wheel*. "They didn't really understand what was being done. They heard funny sounding words, and saw crystals and candles, and they thought that if they just lit a few candles themselves and said some funny words too then they could achieve the same result. Every crystal ball diviner or water dowser you see is doing the same thing as a cargo cult. They're mimicking something real, but they don't understand the meaning behind it."

Alaina picked up a large amethyst crystal off the floor beside her. "This is not just a rock purchased from some hippie crystal shop. This is a fragment from the shattered shrine of Idis. It was tempered with the blood of thousands of sacrifices before the Christians arrived in Denmark and destroyed her visage. These items aren't just for decoration or performance, they're artifacts. Some things have innate power." She placed the amethyst back down on the floor, then reached into the trunk and pulled out a wooden figure. "Other things have power because we've given it to them. An object that brings us comfort, or reminds us of the people we love." Alaina brushed her fingers across the figure's surface. "With it we carry a piece of that person with us, a piece of their guidance, their strength, their love to protect us."

"So, you believe all of these things have power?"

"It's not about what I believe, it's about what is true. Every item in this trunk holds a power that I can tap into. Except the incense, that's just to set the mood."

Loud footsteps crossed the room above them, like someone in heavy boots walking across the wooden floor, followed by a door slamming shut. Hux jumped and growled at the ceiling. "What's going on up there?" Ellie asked.

Alaina shrugged. "I don't know, but I hope they keep it down. I'd like to work on this protection charm, and I'll need to meditate in here for a while. It'll be a lot easier if it's quiet."

Alaina began to arrange the items she had removed from her trunk. "Speaking of quiet." She looked at Ellie.

"Of course, yes, thanks for the chat. I don't think I'm going to find any clues in here anyway."

Ellie and Hux left the parlor. Although Ellie was no closer to understanding the shadow they had captured on camera, she thought maybe she was a little closer to understanding Alaina.

CHAPTER 9

The Bruker House library was a highlight of the estate. Proud shelves of leather-bound books, and ornate woodworking lined the walls. A stained-glass window dominated the far side of the room, the mosaic depicting a woman in white reaching for a golden crescent moon in the night sky. A fireplace along one wall begged for a crackling log, a leather armchair beside the hearth demanded a brooding academic to occupy its seat. A bust of Pallas above the door would not have been out of place.

Ellie walked along the wall and brushed the spines of leather-bound books with her fingertips. There were history collections from every continent and every era, biographies, literary classics, and several ancient and yellowed Bibles. A set of shelves in the back corner held local history and documents. *A History of Northern New England* leaned against a binder of clippings from the *Augusta Recorder*. Yearbooks from Medomak High School spanning nearly a century. A treasure trove of local happenings. Ellie thought if she was to find answers anywhere, it was here.

She pulled a yearbook from the shelf, the spine dated 1954. She flipped through pages of black-and-white faces and names. The smell of leather and old paper filled the air. She closed the book and returned it to the shelf. Her hand landed on *A History of Northern New England*, when Hux pawed at the bottom self.

"What is it, bud?" Ellie bent to see what had captured his interest. Wedged between a stack of *National Geographic* magazines and a *Sibley Guide to Eastern Birds* was a beaten and yellowed baseball. Ellie pulled the ball from between the books and saw that an unreadable signature was scrawled across its leather.

Hux looked up at her, his eyes bright and ready for the throw.

"You can't have this, I'm sorry." Ellie set the ball on a high shelf, beside a book that caught her eye. The spine read *Campbell*. Butterflies erupted in her stomach as she pulled the book from its slot on the bookcase and opened it. Within was page after page of faded Kodacolor prints of the Campbell family. She thumbed through the album and studied it page by page. Family photos from the beach, grandparents, a new car, and most importantly, there was Julie. She blew out candles on a chocolate-frosted cake, a smile crossed her face as she unwrapped gifts on Christmas morning, she sat beside her father on a floral sofa, she had a busted lip. The photos told the story of innocence lost. A young girl, fresh to the world, broken and beaten by it. Beaten by someone who should have kept her safe. A small fire ignited in the pit of

Ellie's stomach, a rage that burned for what had been taken from this young girl.

She landed on a photo of Julie in front of a small cave, a crack in a hillside nearly covered with roots and branches. Like a wound in the earth had opened and struggled to heal. Ellie wondered where the picture had been taken. It was buried among hundreds of family photos in no particular order; vacations were interspersed amid holidays and lazy days at home.

Ellie heard a whisper from behind, and felt cool breath on the back of her neck. The voice's tone was cold and smooth, its words unintelligible. She shut the book and spun around. The library was still and empty.

Ellie's stomach sank like a stone. The tingle of adrenaline spread through her core, its warm electric touch slithering up her spine. "Charlotte?" she called to the empty room.

Beside her Hux stood motionless and stared at the empty fireplace. He let out a long steady whine.

Ellie's legs were as heavy as lead. Her skin went cold. Her eyes darted between every corner, every piece of furniture, desperate to detect that which lurked in the shadows.

Another cold whisper, long and slow. Ellie froze, her heart paused for a beat. A voice spoke from the fireplace.

"Is someone there?" Her voice cracked with fear.

Hux trotted to the fireplace. He looked up at the flue and growled.

Ellie willed her leaden feet to move and she crept toward the stone hearth one small step at a time. Her heart pounded in her chest as she crouched in front of the firebox.

Another whisper, followed by a low round whistle.

After a jolt of panic, the cool breath of relief overcame Ellie. There was no otherworldly presence, no ghosts, no whisperer in the darkness. Only wind down the chimney in a drafty old house.

Ellie pushed the damper shut and stood. She looked down at Hux. "These ghost hunters have me jumping at shadows, and you're no help. Come on, bud, let's get out of here and find something to eat."

———————

ELLIE WATCHED the mid-day sun shine through the dining room's floor-to-ceiling windows. Wavy glass panes cast fractal patterns across the dining table in a slow-motion light show. The room felt old in a way the others didn't. Ellie could imagine the heavy oak table lined with Lords and Ladies, dignitaries from far-off lands, and old money debutantes. Now in their place sat a backwoods nobody from Missouri eating a decadent meal of Wonder Bread and Skippy, dog at her feet.

The room was pristine save for a large red stain on the ceiling. Its chaotic shape spread outward like fingers from the base of a crystal chandelier. The stain had a blood-like appearance, as if the house had been stabbed and was slowly bleeding out. Crimson tendrils reached and clawed across the ceiling in search of evermore white to taint. In reality, it was likely an iron-rich water stain, perhaps from a leaky old water pipe or a steam radiator in one of the bedrooms upstairs.

Ellie had spread the contents of David's manila folder across the table, alongside a few mildew-ridden newspapers from the cellar. She flipped through the Campbell photo album while she ate, trying to piece together the family photos with the police reports and newspaper clippings David had collected.

"Must be the lunch hour," a deep voice said from the dining room doorway. David carried a bowl of soup in his hand. "I was going to ask to join you, but I'm not sure there's any room left at the table," he joked as he cleared a spot across from Ellie, tossing a yellow newspaper aside.

"Sorry, I guess I've spread out a little bit," Ellie said. She took a sip of tea from a mug decorated with shooting stars.

"No worries at all. I'm guessing you found something in the parlor?" David placed a spoonful of soup to his lips and gently blew on it.

"No, actually I just talked with Alaina. I was never going to find anything in there anyway. I did find this in the library though." Ellie passed the Campbell family photo album to David.

"I remember this family, they had a daughter go missing," David said. He flipped through the pages of photos.

Ellie nodded her head. "Julie. I've been trying to put the photos together with some of the reports you collected and these old newspaper articles. I don't know if it'll go anywhere though." She picked at the sandwich on her plate, broke off a piece of crust, and tossed it to Hux.

"Well, you mentioned this morning you were looking for a practical explanation for the disappearances. Who knows, maybe you'll stumble onto something." David shut the photo album and set it on the table. "Find anything else interesting?"

"Not really." Ellie sighed, tired and defeated. She picked more at her half-eaten sandwich. "Actually, now that I think about it, before you called us back to the house, Charlotte and I did find a family plot in the woods. Some of the Brukers are buried out there. It doesn't explain anything, but I thought it might be worth a mention."

David paused while holding a spoonful of soup a half-inch above his bowl. "I did read somewhere that Alexander and Helena were buried on the property. Which way was it? I might check it out later."

"Down the hill past the carriage house, you can't miss it. There's a big obelisk in the center. Most of the graves look the same except for Helena's. Hers has a big slab of granite over top of it."

David stopped eating. "Oh, that's very interesting. I wonder if—"

"You guys need to listen to this!" Charlotte announced as she burst into the room. Startled by the intrusion, Hux jumped and let out a low growl. Charlotte balanced an open laptop in one hand and set it on the table next to David. "I was listening to the EVPs Alaina collected this morning, and I found this."

Charlotte leaned over a chair at an awkward angle and clicked play on an open audio file. White noise streamed from the laptop's tinny speakers. "Is there anyone in the room with me now?" Alaina's quiet breathy voice came through the small speakers much louder than expected. There was another stretch of white noise before Alaina asked another question. "If there is a presence in this room, please identify yourself."

"Listen after the next question," Charlotte said. It was difficult to tell if the tone of her voice held excitement or anxiety, or maybe a mixture of both.

David and Ellie waited in silence while Alaina asked a third question. "What is it you want at Bruker House?" Static crackled followed by a faint voice. Ellie heard a single word that sounded like "upper."

"Did you hear that?" Charlotte asked. Her voice nearly cracked as the words came out. She scrambled to pause the playback as Alaina's voice streamed from the speakers again with a fourth question asking if the presence could make itself known.

"Can you isolate that?" David asked. He was still holding onto a forgotten spoonful of soup.

Charlotte dragged a few bars on the open window and set the playback to repeat. The audio played over and over. "Upper... upper... upper." Hux went rigid. His ears perked in the direction of the sound.

"It sounds like it's saying *suffer*," David said.

Charlotte stopped the playback. "That's what I thought too."

Ellie shook her head and threw up a hand. "It could sound like anything. We're all just hearing what we want to hear. I thought I heard 'upper,' but for all we know it's just the sound of the floor creaking."

"Where was the recording taken?" David asked. He finally gave up on lunch and dropped the spoon back into the bowl of soup.

Charlotte checked the file name of the recording. "Unfinished bedroom – floral wallpaper, taken on digital recorder number three. That's the bedroom at the end of the hall, the one above the parlor."

"Ellie, you've got some ideas for practical explanations, why don't you take a look around the room? See if you can find any creaky floorboards or another way to repeat what we just heard. Charlotte, maybe you can go along with her and take more EVPs, see if this guy's got anything else to say," David said.

"Will do," said Charlotte. She slammed the laptop lid shut and made her way upstairs. Ellie cleaned up what was left of her lunch and followed close behind.

"Let me just grab a recorder real quick," Charlotte said as they walked the long upstairs hallway. She unlocked her guest room and Ellie waited in the doorway while she searched her bag. Ellie saw the vanity mirror in Charlotte's room was covered, a bedsheet had been haphazardly thrown over the glass.

"Got it!" Charlotte said. She held up a digital recorder in her hand as she walked toward the door.

The bedroom at the end of the hall had yet to be renovated and was in relative disrepair compared with the recently refinished rooms. The herringbone floor needed to be sanded and stained, the ceiling plaster was cracked and several chunks had fallen away to expose the lath beneath, decades of dirt and grime collected in each corner, and to top it all off, the decor of the room was among the ugliest in Bruker House. A hideous yellow and green floral print wallpaper adorned the walls. It may have been warm and vibrant when it was new, but it had faded with time into drab misery. Every edge peeled, surrendering its long tenure as guardian of the bare plaster beneath. Other than the disrepair and outlandish wallpaper, the room was entirely unremarkable, empty save for a single rolled-up carpet stored against the back wall.

"Why did you say *suffer?* Are you suffering?" Charlotte asked. She held the digital recorder out in front of her and awaited a response. Hux cocked his head to one side as she asked the question, wondering if it was directed at him. "Are you trying to say we're going to be the ones to suffer?"

Ellie listened to every step Charlotte took as she recorded the EVPs. She wasn't surprised to find there was no smoking gun to explain the sound captured on Alaina's tape. Old houses were noisy. They had creaky floors, squeaky doors, banging pipes, barely any part of an old house was silent, but amidst all the various rattles and clatters, trying to reproduce a specific sound wasn't always so easy.

Ellie's frustration with the investigation was growing. She had expected the others would use every speck of unexplained dust as evidence for the supernatural, but really the burden of proof should lie with whoever makes a claim. She shouldn't need to provide a natural explanation for anything. If the others wanted to claim a disembodied voice had been caught on tape, then they were the ones who needed to prove where it came from.

"Will you say something again for me now?" Charlotte asked. Hux again cocked his head to one side in curiosity. He wagged his tail slowly back and forth across the floor, wiping away the dust from a small wedge-shaped patch.

"Hey, Ellie, take a look at this," Charlotte said. She stared at the gaudy yellow wallpaper.

Ellie had nearly blocked out Charlotte's voice as background noise during the EVP collection, but her change in tone caught Ellie's attention. "What is it?"

"There's something beneath the wallpaper. Right here, look. It's papered over something." Charlotte reached out and touched the wall, brushing one finger down beside a cluster of faded yellow flowers. The fragile old paper nearly disintegrated beneath her touch.

Ellie joined Charlotte by her side and saw the subtle creases in the wallpaper. Beneath the repeating floral pattern was an outline of straight edges slightly offset from the rest of the wall. The lines hidden within the pattern reminded her of Magic Eye illusions that were popular when she was young, and she wondered if she crossed her eyes just right whether the shape beneath the pattern would become clear.

"I think it's a door," Ellie said.

"I think you're right. It's the right size, at least." Charlotte turned to Ellie with a flash of fear written across her face. "Why do you think someone would cover up a door like that?"

Ellie didn't respond. She didn't know why the door might be covered, but the fact it was here at all did lend weight to one of her theories about the missing persons. A hidden door meant Bruker House held secrets, and there may be other hidden places for people to go missing, whether by accident or intentional. Bruker House was a mystery yet to be unraveled, and this room could hold some of the clues.

"We should open it," Ellie said.

"I'll get the others."

It didn't take long for Charlotte to gather the other three.

While the team hadn't been given express permission to make changes to the house, David agreed it was okay to take down the wallpaper since it would likely be removed during renovations anyway.

Lou used a boxcutter to slice long lines through the wall-paper, tracing the outline of the door. Ellie and Charlotte peeled the ancient covering away from the wall. It crumbled and flaked into fragments with every section they removed, as if they were peeling away dry leaves.

"Make sure to wash your hands after this. They used to use arsenic for the green color in old wallpaper," Ellie said.

Charlotte rubbed her hands together to dust them off. "Ah, the good old days, when covering your walls in poison was fashionable. Lead paint, asbestos, now arsenic wallpaper too? No wonder people didn't live as long back then."

Beneath the wallpaper was a flat, wooden door stained in dark brown. The casing had been removed along with the knob and plate so that the door was nearly flush with the wall. If it hadn't been for small gaps at the edges, there would be no hint of its existence beneath the wallpaper. A single wood screw held the door shut where the latch had been, and Ellie's anticipation grew as Lou removed it one slow turn at a time. Finally, once the screw was out, Lou wedged the screwdriver between the door and its jam. Ellie held her breath as he pried it open. The door swung outward, and a damp musty smell drifted out from the space beyond; it smelled old and stale like an ancient tomb that had laid untouched for centuries.

Behind the door was a small dark room without windows or lights, maybe intended as a closet. David lifted a flashlight and illuminated the space. Ellie estimated it was maybe six feet long by six feet wide at most, with walls of wood paneling. At first glance, the closet appeared to be empty save for decades of dust that had collected along the edges of the floor. However, on the back wall, a pattern was etched into the wood, its lines interwoven and folded in on themselves in an endless loop.

Charlotte was the first to break the silence. "What is it? What does it mean? Does anyone recognize it?"

"Alaina, you probably know best. Does it look familiar to you?" David asked.

Alaina took a few steps toward the closet and focused on the pattern. "I don't know this shape."

Charlotte moved her hand in the air outlining the curves with a finger. "It's like a maze."

"Looks like some kind of Celtic knot to me," Lou said.

"I have some books with me, I'll see if I can find anything that looks similar. For now, nobody touch it. In fact, you shouldn't even look at it until we know what it is," Alaina said.

"Yes, do that, let us know what you find." David stared straight at the pattern, ignoring Alaina's suggestion to not look at it. "Lou, can you take a few photos?"

"Sure thing. I'll get a camera from the monitoring station."

"Bruker House gets more and more interesting by the minute," David said.

"You ain't kidding," said Charlotte.

As reluctant as Ellie was to admit it, she had to agree with them. She could at least dismiss the video and audio recordings as digital artifacts, one-off phenomena, glitches. The symbol in the closet, however, was cold hard physical evidence. It was undeniable. It wasn't paranormal evidence by any means—it was just a shape carved into the wood, after all—but Ellie had to admit it was *strange*. A pattern carved into the wall in a closed-off and hidden closet said there was something abnormal in the history of Bruker House, there was something missing from the folder of documents David had collected, and whatever it was, Ellie intended to find it.

CHAPTER 10

Deep orange rays streamed through the west-facing windows of Bruker House. Sprites of dust briefly illuminated as they passed beneath amber wedges of light, then disappeared into the darkness between. Outside, the moon, now nearly full, peaked above the horizon in the east joined by a vanguard of evening stars. Bruker House stood in silent serenity as twilight fell over its domain.

The mystery of Bruker House was a maze from which Ellie Hawthorne had not yet escaped, a Gordian knot that couldn't simply be cleaved, but must be untied one small piece at a time. She had spent the afternoon checking every room in the house for hidden doors, even going so far as to remove every book from the library shelves, half-expecting a bookcase to slide open to reveal a hidden passageway. Despite her efforts, there were no secrets to be found.

Ellie had measured each room and sketched the layout of the home in a notebook. She found that with the hidden closet, every square foot of Bruker House had been accounted for. There were no other hidden rooms, no secret back stairs, no trapdoors leading to an underground dungeon. Twenty-four hours in the house, and she was no closer to explaining the disappearances than she was when pouring over files in her own kitchen.

Exhausted and defeated, she granted herself a break and found Lou and David in the dining room. The two of them sat beside one another in high-back chairs with a tablet placed on the table between them. On the screen, Ellie saw a blown-up image of the symbol they had found in the closet upstairs.

Lou noticed Ellie walk in and glanced down at Hux. "Miss Hawthorne! I do believe I've seen that dog follow your every footstep all day long."

"Like Velcro," Ellie said.

Hux walked over to greet the men and David ruffled his fur. Hux collapsed onto the floor near their feet and let out a heavy sigh.

"I made some pot pie for dinner, it's on the stove in the kitchen. Help yourself if you want some," Lou said. He got up from his seat with a grunt and shuffled to the kitchen.

"Thanks, I might take you up on that. Where's everyone else?" Ellie asked David.

"Charlotte is in the monitoring station, and last I saw Alaina was in her room pouring over a few books of hers. I think we're all pretty intrigued by the meaning of that symbol we found. Lou and I have been trying to make sense of the pattern for God knows how long. We just... can't do it," David said. He motioned his finger around the tablet screen as he spoke, tracing the path of the lines.

"What do you mean?" Ellie took a seat beside David at the dining table, and he slid the tablet in front of her. There, in high definition, was the mysterious pattern. Its lines twisted and folded into a bizarre labyrinthine knot.

"Look here." David hovered a finger above the tablet surface and traced a line. "You can start anywhere you want, but if you follow the pattern when it loops back around, you end up in a different place. It just doesn't make sense. It doesn't seem possible."

Ellie followed the knot's path with her eyes and saw what David had meant. In a Celtic knot design, a line could be followed over and under intersecting lines, then end up in the same place at the end in an infinite loop. In this pattern, as each line traced a path through intersecting lines, it transitioned into negative space. Ellie had seen similar tricks in optical illusions like the Shepard Elephant. "It's just like an M.C. Escher drawing, a trick of expectations and perspective."

"Maybe, but I just can't wrap my head around it," David said. He slid the tablet back in front of himself and stowed it in the same leather satchel he brought with him to Ellie's office on the first day they met. "We'll see if Alaina can find anything like it in her references. I'd love to know what it means, and why someone would go through the trouble to hide it."

Lou shuffled back in from the kitchen with a can of Moxie in his hand. He reclaimed the chair beside David.

"Speaking of that room," Ellie said. "It makes me wonder if there are other parts of Bruker House that we don't know about, and whether it could explain some of the disappearances. I checked the rest of the house today, and I don't think we're missing anything else in the main building, but last night I saw a light outside my bedroom window that I can't explain. I thought it might be coming from an outbuilding, but this morning I searched and couldn't find anything."

"A light? The only other building on the property is the carriage house. Are you sure it wasn't coming from there?" David asked.

Lou cracked open the Moxie can and the tab made a crisp pop. The sound pierced Ellie to the core, and a scream slithered its way out into the open from the deep recesses of her memory. Her mother cradled a broken wrist against her blood-splattered blouse.

"You okay?" David asked.

Ellie shook her head. "I'm fine. It wasn't the carriage house, it's in the wrong direction."

"What did the light look like? What color?"

"It was just a single flickering yellow light, like a candle flame or an old incandescent bulb about to go out."

"Maybe it was a will-o'-the-wisp," Lou said as he took a sip from the can.

"Willow what?" Ellie asked, confused.

"Will-o'-the-wisp," Lou said slowly with a pause between each syllable. "My nan used to tell us stories about them, sometimes she called them a fool's flame. They're spirits or fairies or whatever you want to think of them as. They beckon folks to follow them into the forests or the bogs. Whether their intent is to lead or to mislead depends on who's telling the story, but the way my nan told it, they always led foolish travelers astray. They'd flicker and dance to lead some poor soul deep into the wilderness, then fade away and leave their victim lost in the darkness."

Ellie nodded. "I'm not sure that's the kind of explanation I'm looking for."

"Bit too mystical for you, eh?" Lou asked.

"I guess you could say that."

"I hadn't thought about it in years, but I thought I saw one once, when I was a boy, long long time ago." Lou stared at a spot on the wall and stroked his beard. Hux sat up beside him and whimpered. Lou absent-mindedly reached his hand down and scratched the dog behind the ear. "Used to be I'd walk home from school along Finnegan's Creek near the spot they call The Hollow now. Back in those days they called it The Grove on account of all the trees that used be down that way."

Lou ran his hand across Hux's back and let his fingers disappear into the dog's fur. "One evening I seen a light between the trees, orange light swaying back and forth. I never seen it there before, and my curiosity got the best of me. I didn't believe my old nan's stories anyhow, so I walked toward it. It weren't a fairy, but looking back now, maybe it was a fool's flame. At least, I was a fool. The light was from a lantern, one of them old mining types. Once I saw the man that held it..." Lou took a sip from the can of Moxie. His eyes never strayed from the spot on the wall, and his right hand never left Hux. He continued the story as if he were in a trance. "I don't remember his real name, but us kids used to call him Scabber on account of all the scabs he had on his face. He used to pick at them, and lots of times he'd be bleeding from one or two. He had a reputation around town, used to be a little too interested in us kids. More than a grown man should've been."

Ellie shot a glance to David. A few fingers loosely covered his mouth as he listened to Lou's story.

"I remember him holding the lamp up and asking me to come a bit closer so he could see my face, said all the other boys must be jealous of me on account of I had such a pretty one. Instead of coming closer, I tried to run, but he grabbed me. He was so fast, and his grip was like iron. He grabbed me by the arm at first, but then he started to grab whatever part of me he wanted. He dropped the lantern into the dirt and the flame snuffed out. In the darkness I couldn't see what he was doing, but I felt him, heard his hot, heavy breath heavy in my ear. He was doing things a grown man ought not have been doing with a child, things I wouldn't learn about for a few years afterward."

"My god." David placed a hand onto Lou's shoulder. "I'm sorry something like that happened to you."

The old man seemed to snap out of the trance. He turned his focus away from the spot on wall and lifted his hand from Hux. Lou shrugged. "These things happen."

"No, Lou, what that man did was abhorrent. He violated a child, for Christ's sake. He should've rotted in prison. Did you tell anyone what happened?" David asked.

"I didn't want anyone to know. I hardly told anyone about it my entire life let alone back then. No one talked about such things. Old Scabber probably got to half the kids in town over time. That day I was just the unlucky one. You can't let these things get to you; you just get up, brush the dirt off, and keep on going."

David opened his mouth to speak but said nothing.

Ellie chimed in, "Lou, I don't think it's healthy to just brush off a child molester like that. Who even knows how the trauma affected you."

Lou scoffed. "It was different times. Besides, some good come out of it. Afterward I prayed more and took church a lot more seriously. It brought me closer to the Lord, and eventually I started my own ministry. Maybe that was God's plan all along, and who am I to question Him?"

Loud footsteps walked across the floor above them, and a door slammed shut.

David looked at the ceiling. "The floors sure are thin in this place. That's got be Charlotte. I can't imagine Alaina stomping around like that."

Ellie stayed silent. She had a thousand things to say to Lou about his trauma and his faith, but she held her tongue.

Lou continued. "My point in all this is that my nan was right. Don't go following strange lights. Especially not into the forest, you never know what you might find among the trees." He took a swig of Moxie, then yawned and looked at his watch. "Lordy, I really ought to be getting some shut-eye."

"I'm there with you," David said. "I told Charlotte I'd take over monitoring for her at eleven. I'd love to get a few winks in before then."

"Actually, I'd like to watch the station at some point. If it's okay with you, maybe I could take over for Charlotte?" Ellie said.

"You don't have to do that, Ellie. The overnights can be rough," David said.

"No, I want to do it. I want to feel like I'm doing my part with everyone here."

David crossed his arms and nodded. "All right, meet me there at eleven. It's not too complicated, but I'll show you where everything is and you can take over from there."

———————————

WHITE NOISE FILLED the monitoring station as laptop fans droned. Warm electronics released a hint of ozone that gave the air a clean mechanical odor. The cold unnatural light of computer monitors bathed the room in a blue hue punctuated by flashes of orange and green as LED status lights flickered on and off to prove the machines were hard at work. The electronics of the room performed their tasks without fatigue or complaint while Ellie fought against the urge to sleep.

She looked at the clock on her phone and groaned. It was 3:03am. Eight minutes had passed since she last checked the time, but it had felt like hours. She looked over at Hux curled up on a makeshift bed in the corner. "Only three hours to go, bud," Ellie said. He slowly opened one eye to look at her, then shut it again.

Ellie spun the chair around to face the desk, a folding table hosting a bank of three computer monitors. Each screen was divided into four frames which streamed feeds from the cameras she and Charlotte set up around Bruker House. She took a moment to scan each display and check the feed from all six cameras. Five of them showed nothing but empty rooms; the attic camera flickered to life for a moment then returned to black. She flipped a page in the logbook and jotted down an update. *3am - nothing to report E.H.*

Ellie looked back over the previous log entries and read through a dozen of them before she found anything interesting. It was from the afternoon before. *1pm – left post to use the commode L.T.*

She shook her head and shut the logbook, convinced that manning the monitoring station was a waste of everyone's time. She understood why they did it. David explained they used to collect days' worth of video and watch it back at 5x speed, but they missed things and found that cameras got bumped into odd angles that no one noticed. Now the policy was to have someone watching whenever possible, lest they miss some speck of dust that they could try to pass off as a ghost. Ellie mused that a speck of dust would at least be more interesting than Lou's bathroom breaks.

Hux got up and walked to the center of the room. He stood perfectly still and stared into the open doorway.

"What is it, bud? You hear something?"

Hux did not acknowledge the sound of her voice, he stood in silence, fixated on the empty door frame. Ellie peered into the doorway, but it was too dark to make out anything beyond the threshold. She waited, half-expecting one of the other investigators to round the corner, but there was nothing.

"Hello? Is someone out there?" she called, speaking a little quieter than she intended.

There was no response. She glanced at the cameras, but none of them were angled to capture the hallway outside. She looked back at the empty doorway again; it was pitch black.

"Hello?" she called without response. Hux stood rigid as a statue as he watched the doorway intently.

Ellie got up from the desk and walked toward the open door. She couldn't make out anything in the darkness beyond, so she flicked on her phone's flashlight and pointed it into the hallway. She had expected to at least see the garish wallpaper on the opposite wall, but the phone didn't illuminate a thing. The beam shined into the darkness and faded without landing on a surface, the light tapered off as if it were shining into the deepest depths of the sea.

Ellie's heart thumped a little harder in her chest. She raised her arm and stretched it out into the inky black hallway with a hope that by moving the phone closer to the opposite wall, the light might touch it. She yearned for the comfort of seeing something, anything in the darkness beyond the door. The air in the hallway was cold against her skin. Goosebumps raised on her arm, and she noticed a tremor in her hand. There was not one speck of light in the hallway. As she reached out her hand, the phone and the end of her arm disappeared into a dark fog. It was as if there was nothing in the hallway at all, as if the entire universe had been reduced to the monitoring station, now floating alone in an empty void.

Ellie remembered a light switch along the wall not far from the doorway. She slid her phone back into her pocket, and in a last bastion of hope she reached her hand along the wall and felt for the switch. Although she had no choice but to risk an arm, she didn't dare let the rest of her body leave the illuminated comfort of the room. The air grew colder as she reached her arm farther from the doorway, like she was reaching her hand into a freezer. Finally, her fingers landed on the switch plate. In a moment of panic, she thought nothing would happen, that she would flip the switch and the hall would remain shrouded in darkness. She flicked the switch, and the lights came on. There was the ugly wallpaper across from her, dark hardwood floors, and a runner along the floor. She looked up and down the hallway at rows of doors and sconces. Not a thing was out of place.

Hux sat at her feet. He looked up at her with bright eyes, unfazed by the moments prior.

"You got me all worked up for nothing, you little stinker," she said. His tail gave the slightest hint of a wag.

Ellie switched off the hallway lights and returned to her seat at the desk. She looked back over her shoulder to check the doorway one last time; even with the lights out, she could see the outline of the garish wallpaper on the other side of the hallway.

"You're tired, Ellie. Get a grip," she muttered to herself.

She scanned the feed from each of the cameras again and saw nothing but silent empty rooms and a black void where the attic camera had died. She opened the log and hesitated for a moment as she considered what to write, then made a new addition beneath her previous entry. 3:15am - *nothing to report E.H.*

SLEEP DEPRIVED AND HALFWAY DELIRIOUS, Ellie was struck with an epiphany, an explanation for the shadow they had recorded in the parlor. The cameras around Bruker

House used modern digital sensors and almost certainly captured images with a rolling shutter, which could have strange effects when recording objects in motion. Airplane propellors, lightning strikes, anything quicker than the camera's shutter could be captured as a strange, fragmented version of itself. With a rolling shutter, the shadow they saw move across the room could be explained by variations in lighting between each frame. It could be something as simple as a flickering light.

"Hux, I think we might be on to something," Ellie said.

The dog picked his head up off the makeshift bed, and looked at her inquisitively.

Ellie stood up from the desk and the wheelie chair rolled lazily out from behind her until it stopped against the far wall. "Come on, bud, we might be able to debunk some of this paranormal voodoo after all."

She paused for a moment at the monitoring station doorway. The hallway lights were off, but she could still see the gaudy patterns on the opposite wall. At least in this moment her sanity was intact.

She and Hux made their way down the large ornate staircase into Bruker House's grand entry hall. In the early morning hours, the quiet hall felt like the lobby of an empty theater, ready to be filled by crowds and excitement come showtime. Empty it felt off somehow, uncanny.

In the parlor, Ellie flipped the light switch on the wall, which illuminated a floor lamp in the corner of the room. There was no flicker. She remembered playing with light switches as a child; if she nudged the switch into just the right position, it would make a crackling sound and the room lights would flicker like a strobe. She pressed lightly on the parlor switch and hoped to see the lamp flicker. Nothing. She flipped the switch on and off, gently pressing from both sides and looking for a sweet spot, but there was none.

She kept the light on and walked to the lamp. She jiggled the cord and the bulb. No flicker. She tapped the shade, shook the base, and even pled with the lamp, but it shined bright and consistent. "Shit," Ellie muttered to herself. She needed to reproduce the shadow they captured on camera if she wanted to make a convincing case for her theory. She couldn't get a flicker from the switch, and she couldn't get a flicker from the lamp, so there was only one option that remained. The breaker.

Ellie looked over to Hux, who lay in a leather armchair and watched her strange routine with the lamp. "You'll protect me in the spooky cellar, right?" she asked without a response.

Ellie made her way to the back hall of the house, and to the stairs which led down into the cellar. She pushed open the door and it responded with a slow, consistent whine that didn't taper off until the very end of its arc. The first few steps into the cellar were illuminated by the hall light while the rest of the staircase disappeared into a black abyss. Not quite as black as the upstairs hallway had seemed, but close.

The cold damp air of the cellar sucked heat away from Ellie's body. She wrapped her arms across her chest to try to keep warm. At the bottom of the staircase, she found the pull chain to turn on the cellar lights and gave it a gentle tug. Dim light from several scattered bulbs flooded most of the cellar. The cave-like structure in the back remained dark, Ellie could hear the steady drip of water as it splashed onto the stone floor like an ominous metronome. A voice within her said she should leave it be, that to use her phone's flashlight to reveal whatever might be in the cave was to invite answers to a question she didn't want to ask. So she ignored it and focused on the breaker.

The electrical boxes were hung along the far wall and, to Ellie's relief, she found that they were brand new and meticulously labelled. She made a mental note to thank Hank when he returned. Inside the first box, Ellie found a row labelled *Kitchen, dining room, parlor outlets*. She didn't have the benefit of being in the parlor itself to see if the lights flickered, so she touched the breaker gently at first, harder after a few moments, then jiggled it back and forth. She estimated the amount of force she applied could reasonably happen on its own from natural contraction and expansion throughout the day.

"Well, bud, let's see if we made ourselves a shadow monster." Ellie looked over to Hux, who was sniffing along one of the cellar walls. He paused and looked up at the sound of her voice, unsure of why they had embarked on this adventure.

Ellie shut the breaker box and made her way back to the pull chain lightbulb. She reached up and wrapped her hand around the chain, then looked over at the cave, its dark opening like the throat of a massive creature, unwelcoming, featureless and devoid of warmth.

She was secure in her conviction that there was nothing supernatural in Bruker House, nothing supernatural anywhere, nothing in the darkness that wasn't there in the light, but some part of her brain screamed to leave the light on. It felt safe, and familiar, and in darkness lay the unknown. She released her hand from the pull chain and lied to herself; she would leave the cellar light on in case she needed to come back down and wiggle the breaker again. No other reason. It was the lie one told themselves to maintain a consistent internal narrative, to avoid the discomfort of cognitive dissonance.

Ellie and Hux hiked back up the cellar stairs to the main floor and then up again the grand staircase to the monitoring station to vet their success. After some searching on one of the laptops, Ellie found the video playback option in the camera recording software. She dragged the cursor to just after she and Hux left the parlor, then waited and watched. She tried to imagine what she and Hux were doing as each minute ticked by, down the cellar steps, light bulb on, and then she saw it. A shadow moved across the camera feed nearly identical to the one they'd captured the previous day. Internally, Ellie cried out in satisfaction; externally, she clenched a fist and whispered just above her breath, "Yes!" Here was a rational physical explanation for the so-called *shadow creature*. It was an undiagnosed case of flickering lights.

Ellie ruffled the fur on the back of Hux's head. "Couldn't have done it with you, bud. One point for science, zero for voodoo bullshit."

While Ellie felt triumphant in the moment, a small part of her regretted that she would need to break the news to the other investigators. They were all excited to capture something on camera so early, and her new finding would crush that. While it felt good to prove that the world was rational and physical once again, she couldn't help but feel like a wet blanket intent on ruining the party. A small part of her considered keeping the finding to herself. *So what if people want to believe in the supernatural?* she asked herself. *Where's the harm in it?* She considered it for only a moment, then let it pass. It was her duty during this investigation, and as a woman of science in general, to find physical models to explain phenomena, to be rational and open-minded, and to be honest with data. Ellie took her role seriously, and in the morning, she would pass her findings on to David and the other investigators.

Ellie looked at the clock. 4:20am. She made a note in the logbook and returned to watching the monitors.

CHAPTER 11

Five o'clock rolled around and signs of life began to stir in Bruker House. Lou was the first one up. Ellie heard him leave his guest room and watched the video stream as he shuffled down the grand staircase and crossed the hall toward the kitchen. Next was David, around five thirty, who followed Lou's path. At ten before six, Ellie watched David walk back up the stairs with one hand on the railing, and a mug of coffee in the other. A knock on the monitoring station doorjamb followed shortly after.

Hux left his makeshift bed in the corner and walked over to greet David with a gentle wag of his tail. David ruffled the dog's ears and the fur of his head. "Let me guess, you were visited by three ghosts last night, and you're ready to change your ways and admit this place is haunted," David said with a smile.

Ellie laughed. "Close! Except exactly the opposite. I didn't see anything supernatural last night, and I have an explanation for our shadow monster."

145

David raised his eyebrows as he took a sip of coffee. "Oh? Let's hear it."

"Do you know what a rolling shutter is on a camera?"

David shook his head.

"Come check this out." Ellie waved David over to the desk and showed him the clip of the shadow she reproduced the night before. She explained the rolling shutter effect and how a flickering light was able to produce the image they'd seen.

"So, what you're saying is, it was just an illusion? An artifact of digital cameras?"

"Basically, yes."

"Well, I'll be damned. Incredible work, Ellie! You just might be the next Henry Weiss after all!" David blew on his coffee, sending fingers of steam swirling before him, before taking a sip.

Ellie gave a half-hearted bow. "I don't know if I'd go quite that far, but I'll take the compliment. I was worried the news would be a bit of a downer."

"It is a bit, but we've still got another full day of investigation ahead of us. If you don't mind, could you write up your explanation so that I can include it in my report? I want to make sure I have all the facts straight."

"Yes, of course, I'll do it later today after I get some rest."

David took another sip from his mug, then sat down on the floor against the wall and shut his eyes. Hux padded over and laid his head in David's lap. "I feel like I just can't get any sleep in this damn house. I've had so many strange dreams."

"Why's that? See a ghost?"

David let out a sigh. "Something like that."

"Really?"

"Yes, but not here. It happened a long time ago. It isn't a very pleasant story, but if you aren't too tired, I'll tell it to you."

"Less pleasant than the one about the murdered boy?"

"Pretty similar actually." David scratched Hux's head as the dog settled into a comfortable spot.

"Don't you have any warm fuzzy stories you could tell instead?"

David smiled and shook his head. "Not as many as I'd like to have, that's for sure."

"All right then, let's hear it."

David took another sip from his mug and set it down on the floor beside him. He ran a hand along Hux's back through his mottled fur. "You have to understand, this story is from a dark time in my life. I'm not the same man now that I was then."

Ellie nodded.

David took a deep breath. He leaned his back against the wall and shut his eyes. "I served in Desert Storm as a young man, saw things there that no person should have to see. Some of those things, once they get into your head, they just...don't seem to want to let go. Back in those days, the Army didn't take PTSD as seriously as they do now, and, well, I started looking for help at the bottom of a bottle. When I first started drinking, it was just an occasional thing, but it didn't take long before it became an everyday thing. We all have our preferred drink, and for me it was a whisky called Kentucky Choice." David opened his eyes and looked at Ellie. "You remember that cheap trash? It came in those little plastic bottles with a buffalo on the front."

Ellie felt a jolt of electricity at David's mention of Kentucky Choice. It was a brand she knew all too well. It was her father's pick too. Old Jack Hawthorne loved that bottom-shelf swill. The floor of their little trailer would be littered with empty bottles, little paths of open floor weaved between the piles with just enough space to walk. It would stay that way until some random switch flipped in Jack's head and he decided the mess needed to be cleaned. Of course, he never lifted a finger to pick up a single bottle himself; instead, he'd beat Ellie's mother and then stand over her while she cleaned up every last one. Sometimes he'd even hide a few of them to make sure she checked every spot, and if she missed any, he'd dump out every bag and make her pick them all up again. Ellie remembered the smell of the cheap whiskey. She was normally noseblind to it, but after staying overnight with a friend she would come home and be blasted with the stench as soon as she opened the door. She used to wonder if she smelled the same way, if she would walk onto the school bus each morning and all the other kids smelled the putrid sour stench of a hundred moldy bottles of Kentucky Choice.

"I've heard of it," Ellie said.

"God, I loved that stuff. The weight of the bottle in my pocket as I carried it home from the liquor store, the way I sipped it and held it in my mouth before swallowing. I had the whole process down, and I swear the ritual of it all was even more addicting than the drink itself. There's a comfort in it, doing it the same way every time. Anyway, before I knew it, drinking became the only thing I would look forward to, it was all that mattered in my life at that point. I had nothing else. One Saturday night after a day spent drinking at home, I hopped into my truck to buy some more. It wasn't the first time I drove like that; I did it all the time. Hell, I was drunk all the time. I thought nothing of it."

David paused and took another sip of his coffee. He looked at the floor and shook his head. "That day it all caught up with me though. I made a turn—speeding, of course—and this kid was playing in the street. I don't know what he was doing there, but I was so slow to react. I didn't even notice the boy until the truck was already on top of him. I still remember the sound his body made as I hit him, a squishy thump, and the way the suspension swayed back and forth as he went under the tires."

David looked up at her, and Ellie could see the pain written on his face. "Eventually I slammed on the brakes, but it was way too late. I just sat in the truck for God knows how long until I finally had the courage to look in the rearview mirror. I saw his body lying there in the street. He wasn't moving, but I told myself maybe I just knocked him out, that he'd be back up in no time; kids were bouncy, after all. I got out of the truck, and as I walked toward the body I saw blood pooling around him. I can still see it in my head as if it were yesterday. It spread out in a nearly perfect circle, so dark in the evening light that it looked like used motor oil. Then I saw his face, and it was worse than anything I saw in Desert Storm. Way worse. His mouth was agape and twisted at an angle that shouldn't be possible for a jaw. One cheek was all crumpled in and an eye was hanging out of the socket, held on by only a few strands of flesh. The rest of his body was a

149

bloody mess, with limbs bent in ways they weren't meant to bend. I hit him so hard I knocked out one of his eyes. Didn't even tap the brake. Jesus, just think about that." David shook his head and looked back down at the floor.

Ellie raised a hand to her mouth.

"I'm sorry, I shouldn't go into the gory details. That part of the story isn't what you asked about. After the accident, I spent a year in county and got clean while I was in, but I was haunted by what I'd done. I used to dream about that boy all the time, I'd see his mangled face and his twisted body lying in the road. He'd always lift one shattered arm and point at me. He never got up, he never said anything, he just pointed. Then one night I woke up from one of the dreams and there he was, standing in the doorway to my bedroom. He just stared at me with that crushed and bloody face. He didn't point though, he just turned and walked away. I was petrified, of course. I was scared shitless and I couldn't move. Eventually, I pulled myself out of bed and followed him into the hall. I thought maybe he wanted to show me something, but he was gone. I never saw him again after that, and I rarely dreamt of him either. It was almost like he had decided it was time to leave. Until recently, that is. The last few nights, he's been in my mind a lot. I keep dreaming about that window out front, and about that boy."

"I'm so sorry, David. I didn't know you'd been through all that."

David sighed. "It was a long time ago. Thankfully I'm a different man now. A better man I'd like to think."

"You're right, you are. Thank you for telling me your story, I'm sure it wasn't easy."

David nodded. "I'm sure you don't believe I saw him though. The ghost, I mean."

Ellie shook her head. "You're right, I don't. I mean, I think you saw him in your mind, but I don't think he was actually there. It could be something like sleep paralysis, or just a very vivid dream. You were having dreams of him already anyway."

"I know it might sound like that. It's hard to describe, but I know it wasn't a dream. Like you said, I dreamt of him many times, but this time was different. He was there that night, I'm as certain of that as I am that you're here with me now."

Ellie nodded. "I appreciate you telling me your story."

David got to his feet, grunting as he stood. "You're welcome, but now I should take over the station, and you should get some sleep."

ELLIE LAY down in the formidable four-post bed, her head cradled by a cool pillow, and Hux curled at her feet. She sunk into the deep black waters of sleep.

She was running, but from what she couldn't remember. She looked behind and saw nothing, a darkness so deep that it felt endless. Ahead of her was a dim light. As she ran toward it, she saw she was in a tunnel, the walls narrowed until the craggy stone of the passage was barely wide enough for her to fit through. She slowed to a jog, and finally to a walk.

The passage was cold and dark, the ground thick with mud. The orange pulsating glow ahead drew ever closer, just visible beyond the jagged rock faces which lined the narrow passageway. Deeper in the tunnel, the muddy ground was flooded with icy water, at first only an inch deep, but soon deep enough to reach midway up her calves. The cold caused her feet to ache, and her ankles groaned with every step. She shuffled through the freezing water and crept toward the ever-brighter glow, ducking and contorting her body to squeeze between the narrow rock. A fissure in the earth, a crack in the hillside.

The tunnel opened into a small circular space, stacked stone lined the walls and arched upward like a neolithic dome. The walls were lined with dozens of flickering candles. Gentle flames licked at the stones and illuminated hundreds, maybe thousands of symbols scrawled across the walls of the cavern. The glyphs danced and swayed in the flickering shadows of the candlelight. She saw that she wasn't alone. A cloaked figure stood in the back of the space and basked in the amber glow. It stood with its arms outstretched above a desiccated corpse laid upon a large stone slab. The body's brown skin was pulled taut against the bone, so dry that it might flake away in a light breeze. The corpse's eyes had dried and crumbled to leave vacant sockets; its lips were pulled back into an unsettling sardonic sneer that straddled the gap between amusement and pain.

The cloaked figure turned and revealed a face that Ellie recognized. Helena Bruker looked only somewhat older than she had in the photo David shared, but her sharp features and stern face were unmistakable. She placed a single white candle onto the flat stone beside the mummified corpse and lit it with a match, then opened a leather-bound book beside it. She dipped two fingers into a brass bowl and used the red liquid within to paint symbols across the forehead of the body. She referenced the book for each character—first a spiral, then a stylized triangle, then several more complex shapes that Ellie couldn't quite make out. Helena Bruker caressed the cheek of the corpse and stared into the vacant pits that once held eyes. She bent over and kissed the corpse's grimacing mouth, her lips and tongue slid across the bare teeth, and dry fragments of what used to be skin flaked away.

Ellie turned, unsure that she wanted to watch any more of the macabre act, but the passage behind her was a black void. There was nowhere else to look but toward the light.

Helena unclasped her cloak and let it fall from her shoulders. She was bare beneath save for dozens of symbols scrawled across her body in red pigment. She looked directly at Ellie with empty lifeless eyes and pointed at the corpse. "He died screaming," she said flatly. Her eyes unwavering, she reached a finger up and pointed at Ellie. "You'll die screaming too."

Ellie's heart pounded. She turned to run, but her limbs were heavy and lethargic, every motion was slow.

Black ink flooded into Helena's eyes, and her mouth opened wide. She let out a cold and inhuman wail. A single finger remained fixated on Ellie as inky tendrils erupted from the pitch-black voids of Helena's face. Black hands reached from the walls of the cave and clawed at Ellie, scratching and groping her. She screamed for her body to move, but every muscle responded in slow motion. Helena Bruker's scream amplified as her body began to evaporate, as did the mummified corpse, as did the cavern itself. Piece by piece, the tunnel faded away and melted into the abyss until Ellie was left alone in a void with Helena's siren call.

The piercing wail faded into the darkness, and was replaced by cries from Charlotte as Ellie woke.

"Help! Somebody!" Charlotte called, her voice choked with fear.

Ellie had no time to change out of her sweat-soaked night clothes. She jumped out of bed and threw open the bedroom door. Before she could stop him, Hux bolted out of the room and up the hall toward Charlotte's voice, now joined by David's as well.

Lou was sprawled out across the hallway floor, limp and unconscious.

CHAPTER 12

Charlotte knelt beside Lou and held his right hand in hers. She mumbled reassurances to him about how he was going to be okay, and how they were going to get him help. David had two fingers pressed against Lou's neck to check for a pulse; he bent his head low and put his ear to Lou's mouth. Farther down the hall, Ellie saw Alaina standing, her right hand covering her mouth while the other crossed her chest. She glanced from Lou up to Ellie with wide eyes; tear tracks ran down both sides of her face.

"Anything?" Charlotte asked David, her grip tight on Lou's hand.

"What happened?" Ellie asked. She knelt beside Charlotte and held Hux back from the commotion.

"He's breathing, but his pulse is all over the place," David said. "We need to get him to a hospital ASAP."

Alaina let out a squeak from behind her hand-covered mouth.

Charlotte dropped Lou's hand and pulled her phone out

of her pocket. "Does anyone have service?" She looked around in desperation, but she already knew the answer.

"We need to get him down the hill ourselves," David said. "Can you guys help me get him downstairs?"

Ellie and Charlotte each grabbed one of Lou's legs while David slid his arms beneath Lou's shoulders. David counted to three, and together they lifted. It took all of Ellie's strength to get her portion off the ground. Even taking less than a third of Lou's weight, she was shocked at how hard it was to carry an unconscious man.

David grunted as he struggled with the bulk of the weight. "Alaina, can you help lift his mid-section?"

Alaina shook her head, and backed away.

David shot her a look of disgust.

Tears streamed down Alaina's face as she slid back against the wall. "I can't, I can't touch him," she choked out between sobs.

"The three of us can do it," David said between gritted teeth. He nodded for them to start walking, and they carried Lou down the grand staircase one small step at a time, careful not to let his weight shift off balance.

In the foyer, they gently laid Lou down onto the oriental rug. All three of them were winded, Ellie's arms felt like gelatin.

David pulled a set of car keys from his pocket and spoke between breaths. "I'll back the van up to the front steps, get it as close as I can." He opened the front door and jogged out onto the porch and down the steps.

Charlotte knelt beside Lou and placed her hand over his heart. "You'll be all right, we're going to get you the help you need." She looked up at Ellie. "I don't know how long he was out. I was just coming back from checking the trail cams, and I found him lying there. I know he has heart issues, but he takes medicine for it."

Ellie put a hand on Charlotte's shoulder. "He'll be okay. We'll get him to a hospital." A steady beep sounded outside as David reversed the van.

Charlotte nodded, but tears welled in her eyes as reality hit her. "He's seventy-six years old, cher, and the hospital's so far. Why's it have be so far?" She spoke the words quietly, as if Death may hear her if she spoke them too loud.

David burst through the front door. "All right, let's get him in the back."

The three of them lifted Lou again. Ellie's arms screamed, and it took everything she had to keep a grip on him. They waddled across the porch, then David stepped into the back of the van and pulled Lou in while Ellie and Charlotte pushed.

David took off his sweater, rolled it up, then gently placed it beneath Lou's head. "He should be okay back here. I'll call the paramedics as soon as I have a signal and see if they can meet me someplace. I'll come back as soon as he's stable."

"Don't you need one of us to come with you?" Charlotte asked.

David shook his head. "No, I can get him to help on my own. You stay here and take care of the others. I'll be back as soon as I can."

"You take good care of him," Charlotte said as she shut the van's door.

David pulled the van through the front gates and down the hill toward town. He drove as fast as he dared on the pothole-ridden road, which unfortunately wasn't very fast at all.

"He'll be okay, he's in good hands," Ellie said.

Charlotte was silent as she watched the last glimpse of David's van disappear between the trees. Without a word, she hugged Ellie and held the embrace, then walked back up the steps and through the front doors of Bruker House. Somehow the house's facade seemed bigger to Ellie, more imposing than it appeared when she first arrived. Maybe it was she who felt smaller.

Ellie noticed she was alone in the courtyard. In all the commotion, she had lost track of Hux. The dog who was normally glued to her side was nowhere to be seen. "Hux?" she called, hoping to see him bound around a corner. The courtyard was still, silent, save for the far-off drone of the van's engine.

She walked up the porch steps and back inside the house. A sour smell hung in the air of the foyer. She wondered what had been cooked to make the house smell so strange.

"Hux?" she called. She waited for a moment, but he didn't come. "Huxley! Come here, bud!" she called louder. A pang of fear rumbled inside her.

Ellie threw open the door to the study. The room was empty, but she called for Hux all the same. She checked the library next; the room was silent and still. Scenarios raced through her mind. What if he was lost? Hurt? What if he had become the twelfth victim, gone to wherever Julie Campbell, the Brukers, and so many others had gone before?

In the parlor, Ellie found Charlotte lying on a chaise longe. She stared at the ceiling with her fingers interlaced across her stomach, as if preparing to recite her life story to a psychiatrist. "Is Hux in here with you?" Ellie asked with a little less composure than she intended.

Charlotte turned her head, and Ellie saw her eyes were wet with tears. "No. I heard you call for him, he didn't come?"

"No, it isn't like him."

Charlotte sat up. "Want me to help you look?"

"Let me check upstairs first, maybe he got locked in my room."

Ellie made her way up the grand staircase and called again. Panic festered within her. A small voice told her that when she crested the stairs and saw the spot where Lou had lain sprawled on the floor, she would find Hux's body there in his place. Her heart pounded in her chest; she dreaded what she might find as she rounded the corner to the hallway.

There he was. Not sprawled across the floor, but laying beside Alaina with his chin resting on her lap. Alaina still sat against the wall beside where they found Lou, staring into her lap and absent-mindedly scratching Hux behind his ears.

"You had me so worried," Ellie said as she sat beside Hux. He glanced up at her and wagged his tail, but he didn't raise his head from Alaina's lap.

Alaina looked up at Ellie. Her eyes blistered red and her pale face was streaked with tears. Her lip quivered.

"We got Lou into the back of the van and David is driving down the hill as we speak. I think he'll be okay." Ellie scooted against the wall beside Alaina and scratched Hux's back.

Alaina shook her head and fresh tears dripped down her nose. "No, he won't be."

"We don't know—"

"I do know!" Alaina said. She started sobbing and struggled to get any more words out.

Ellie put her hand on top of Alaina's and was shocked at how cold it was. The woman's skin felt like she had just pulled her hand out of a freezer.

Alaina pulled away from Ellie's touch. She took in two deep breaths to settle down before she tried to speak again. "We talked for a while last night. He told me about his wife and family, and his time in the church. I finally got up to go to bed, he said, 'See you in the morning,' and I knew it right then. I knew those would be the last words I'd ever hear him speak."

Alaina trembled. She pulled Hux a little closer and wrapped her arms around him. He let out a sigh. Ellie could see that being hugged by a near-stranger was low on his list of favorite things. Like all dogs, though, he had a sense for when a person needed comfort, and a warm soul like his was always willing to answer the call.

Alaina wiped her face with the sleeve of her sweater. She had settled down, and her words came out easier. "I had the same feeling right before my dad died. I didn't understand what it meant back then. I didn't know how to interpret the feelings I had, but I still felt them." She looked vacant as she told the story, staring straight ahead as she spoke. It was as if she were watching a memory play out like a movie, narrating what happened on screen instead of having lived it. "I was only seven. One night my dad put me to bed just like any other. He read a story and said good night, but something in me, something deep within me, felt wrong. Like a darkness was coming. I knew something awful was going to happen, and I can't explain how, but I just knew that I'd never hear his voice again. I wanted to cry out, or to run to him and throw my arms around him, but I didn't. I lay there in bed awake all night, waiting for that dark cloud to come. The next morning, I found him in the kitchen, face down on the floor. His body was sprawled out like a rag doll. He looked just like Lou did."

Alaina's voice choked, but no more tears came. She held Hux close and let her hands wander through his fur. "I touched him. I touched my dad's body as it was sprawled out across the floor. I felt the cold emptiness of it. All the warmth, and spirit, and love I normally felt was gone. There was nothing left of him, it was just an empty body on the floor, like a house without a family, left vacant and decaying. That feeling never left me. It's like when I felt that empty shell that used to be my father, a part of myself became empty along with it. Like whatever part of his love and kindness should have stayed with me was taken."

Alaina let go of Hux and looked Ellie in the eyes. "I'm sorry I couldn't help carry him. I just couldn't bear to feel emptiness like that again."

Ellie nodded and searched for words to respond to Alaina, but she found no words of comfort to give. "It's okay, I think he would understand. For what it's worth, I hope you're wrong."

"Me too," Alaina said. She looked down into her lap and

played with her bracelet. "I haven't been feeling myself lately. I think I need to be alone for a while."

Ellie nodded. "I understand." She stood and Hux followed.

———

GREY CLOUDS BROUGHT MID-AFTERNOON RAIN, and the shadow they cast over Bruker House suited the dark mood of the day. Ellie wondered if Lou had made it to a hospital in time, if David was still with him or on his way back, maybe the van had run off the road before they even made it back to town. There was no way to know; her phone was a black brick. The isolation of Bruker House felt unnatural in an age of instant communication.

To keep her mind off Lou, Ellie sat at the desk in her room and flipped through her collection of documents. Moldy newspapers, the Campbell photo album, and David's manila folder lay in a haphazard array. She had nearly memorized the smattering of documents and photos, yet was no closer to finding any answers. Bruker House was a jigsaw puzzle with the edges filled in, but now the box was empty and there were no more pieces left to fill in the gaps.

Ellie looked at Hux. "I was crazy to think I could find out what happened to those people. If a dozen detectives across the decades couldn't do it, how could I?" The dog stared and wagged his tail, waiting to hear one of his favorite words.

She peeled a photo of Julie out from beneath a paperclip. The young girl sat atop a brass bed and stared into the camera with lifeless eyes. Her black and blue face was framed by a hideous yellow and green floral print wallpaper. Ellie's mouth dropped open. She turned to Hux. "It was her room."

Ellie walked the long upstairs hallway, photograph in hand, until she reached the unfinished bedroom. She held the photo up and compared the print side-by-side against the wall. There it was: Julie's bedroom and the room with the hidden closet were one and the same. Ellie wondered how many others had slept in this room over the years, feet away from a hidden closet. Perhaps all the missing persons had slept there.

They had found one hidden space in the room, Ellie needed to know if they had missed anything. She felt along the walls and floor, but there were no signs of another hidden passage. She pried open the closet door and entered the musty space beyond. The strange symbol loomed above her as she felt the floorboards and the wall panels. None were loose.

Ellie wondered how it fit together and what she could be missing. If she was missing anything at all. She had found another puzzle piece but wasn't yet sure where it would fit.

She made her way downstairs to think over a cup of tea, Hux followed close at her heels. Bruker House was eerily empty with Lou and David gone. In the quiet she felt like an intruder, like she had broken into a stranger's home to snoop through their belongings. Here she crept through a place that didn't belong to her, to inspect it and pass judgment on its nature. She wondered, if the house were given any say, whether she would be welcome there at all.

Ellie found Charlotte in the dining room and was relieved to see another soul in a house which now felt so unwelcoming. She sat near the head of the table hunched behind a laptop. With her headphones on, she didn't notice Ellie as she walked into the room. Behind her droplets of rain pattered against the bay window; some stayed in place, decorating the glass like flecks of glitter, while others drew blurred lines down each pane on their journey toward the ground.

The red stain loomed above Charlotte. Deep crimson fingers stretched from one wall to the next, reaching, clawing ever farther. Whatever was leaking upstairs had gotten worse, as the red tendrils grew to cover most of the ceiling. Like pooling blood, it soaked into the white fabric of the plaster. Ellie hated to look at it, it was like watching a seeping wound that refused to close.

Charlotte looked up from her laptop without a word. The skin around her eyes was red and raw, her lips showed no hint of a smile.

"Listening to EVPs?" Ellie asked.

Charlotte typed a few words on the laptop before she pulled the headphones down around her neck. "No, reviewing trail cam footage. Trying to keep myself busy, you know?"

Ellie nodded. "I do know."

"Come over here, check this out." Charlotte pulled out the chair beside her and beckoned Ellie to sit. She reluctantly took a seat beneath the seeping stain. Hux collapsed at her feet.

Charlotte passed over the headphones and clicked play on the laptop. At first Ellie only heard static as she watched an empty forest, then a small bird flew into frame and landed on a tree branch, its brown plumage blending in seamlessly against the trees. The bird called, and small puffs of breath bloomed from its beak into the cold air. It sang a song that Ellie had heard a dozen times before, but she couldn't name the bird if her life was at stake.

"What is it?" Ellie asked.

A smile finally crossed Charlotte's lips as she watched the bird sing. "Isn't he beautiful? He's a whippoorwill, cute little guy. In the cold it's almost like you can see his song as the notes slowly drift away. I've been hearing him singing out there since we got here. I'm glad I finally found him."

Ellie took off the headphones and handed them back to Charlotte. "He is very cute, but he's no Bigfoot."

Charlotte shrugged and turned her focus back to the laptop screen. "You jest, but I may find my prize yet, cher."

Ellie glanced up at the red stain. It hung above her, watched her. She thought that if a bead of red-tinted water were to drip on her, she would scream. "Isn't it strange that the contractors have been renovating this place, but it's almost like they missed some spots?"

Charlotte thought for moment before she responded. A gust of wind splattered rain against the window and the drops crackled like a snare fill. "You know, I was thinking that too, just small things here and there. Maybe they think the blemishes are what gives the house character? Like that beautiful library full of books. I was going to sit in there today, but there was a big, discolored spot on the wall that bothered me. It reminded me of things I didn't want to think about."

"Like what?" Ellie asked.

Charlotte shut the laptop. "It was terrible finding Lou this morning, lying there on the floor, but if I'm being honest, it ain't what's been at the forefront of my mind today. Ever since we've been here, I've been having dark thoughts and terrible dreams, awful stuff. I know you don't believe this kind of thing, but I think it's the house. I think something about the house is bringing out my darkest thoughts."

Ellie nodded. "I wasn't going to say anything, but I've been having some really vivid dreams too."

"Really?"

"I'm sure it's just stress though. We're in a strange place, isolated, under pressure to find answers. There's a lot going on, and it's not crazy to think it would affect our sleep."

Charlotte shook her head. "No no, it isn't that. I've been on a lot of investigations over the years and I'm rarely bothered by them. It's different here. It feels different."

Hux rested his chin on Charlotte's lap. She stroked the fur behind his ears as she spoke. "Remember I told you I was assigned male at birth?"

Ellie nodded.

Charlotte looked down at the closed laptop and traced her finger around the logo on the lid. "For the longest time I used to hate myself. Before I transitioned, I used to look in the mirror and hate the body I saw there. The disgust I had when I saw myself, I can't even describe it. Since I transitioned, I've always loved looking in the mirror. I love the person I see there. I love her confidence, her beauty, her mind, body, and spirit. All of it. Everything. In this house though... I don't know what it is, but every time I look at a mirror in this house, all I see is the negative parts of myself, mental and physical."

"I saw the mirror in your room was covered."

Charlotte nodded. She ran her fingers through Hux's speckled fur, down his head and across his back. "I couldn't stand to look at myself. Every time I looked in that mirror I kept seeing this." Charlotte peeled down the top of her blouse and pointed to a circular scar above her left breast. "When I was in college, early days of my transition, a group of men attacked me. They followed me home, they spit on me and called me a faggot, they kept trying to lift up my skirt and grope me. Then when they got tired of tormenting me, they beat me." Charlotte struggled to get the last words out, tears welled in her eyes.

Ellie took Charlotte's hand in hers. "My God, Charlotte, I'm so sorry."

Charlotte wiped tears from the corners of her eyes and sniffed. She composed herself with a deep breath and waved a dismissive hand. "I'm okay. Once they had their fill of beating me and groping me, one of the men put out a cigarette on my chest, right here." She pointed to her scar. "All the other wounds faded with time. The bruises healed, gashes closed, their vile words fell away and were forgotten. Everything. Except for this one spot. This mark stayed. For a long time I tried to cover it up, then for a while after that I saw it as a badge of honor, like a battle scar to show what I had overcome. Then I stopped thinking about it altogether. To be honest, it hadn't crossed my mind in years, still there but invisible. Ever since we came to this house, though, it's all I see. I've dreamt of those men every night since we've been here. In my dreams they beat me again and again."

Ellie hugged Charlotte, who lifted her hand from Hux to

wrap both arms around Ellie. "What happened to you was terrible, and you're so much more than that," Ellie said.

Charlotte dried her eyes and nodded. "Thank you, cher. It's just, there's something about this place, you know? Something different. And that spot on the wall in the library, it reminds me of this." She tapped the scar on her chest. "It's like the house is scarred in the same way that I am."

Ellie nodded and took Charlotte's hand in hers.

"What about your dreams?" Charlotte asked. "What have they been about?"

Ellie hesitated. She thought about all the ways she could lie, all the ways she could get out of telling her story. Then she thought about what Alaina had told her in the parlor, that her childhood trauma could have been written on her forehead.

"You don't have to say if you don't want to," Charlotte said as she picked up on Ellie's hesitance.

"No, it's okay. I just need to think about where to start."

Hux put his front feet on Ellie's chair, and she invited him up to sit with her. She hugged him close and with a big sigh he settled into a spot on her lap. "I've been dreaming a lot about something that happened when I was a kid. I grew up in this small town in Missouri called Fredrick's Bluff."

Charlotte nodded. "I remember you saying that."

"It was just a little farming community in the middle of nowhere. A dead town full of dead people. My father was one of them. Old Jack Hawthorne. He had a small piece of land and parked a broken-down trailer on it that we called home. That place wasn't a home so much as a hovel. That trailer was barely suitable to house animals, and for years we lived like animals. Every few months, the power would get shut off because we didn't pay the bill; somehow there was always money for the booze though."

Ellie shook her head and let out a huff of air. "The floor of the trailer would be littered with empty bottles of his rat piss swill. Bottom-shelf shit called Kentucky Choice. Whenever he finished one, he would just leave it wherever it fell. Until he decided there were too many empty bottles lying around, and then he'd beat my mother for letting the trailer get that way. I hated that piece of shit, he was a cruel and stupid man. My mother would always have some excuse for him too. She'd say, 'Your father provides for us,' or, 'He has his demons, but think of all the good things he does.' For the longest time I hated her for it too; hell, maybe I still do. If she had been a stronger woman, she would have taken me away from that place, away from him, but she wasn't. If she ever had the strength, it had been beaten out of her years ago by good old Jack. I'm sure she was an amazing woman at some point, but by the time I knew her, all the joy and dignity was gone. She didn't even seem like a real person anymore, just any empty shell where a person used to be. Dead inside. A dead person full of dead dreams."

Charlotte put her hand on Ellie's arm. "I'm so sorry, cher. No child should have to grow up like that."

"Thankfully, I managed to get out of there. I went to live with my aunt and uncle when I was twelve." Ellie ran her fingers through Hux's fur and felt his warmth. "It was because of a dog, believe it or not. The school bus would stop about a half-mile from the trailer, and one day as I was walking home from the bus this dog came bounding out of the woods. He was a heeler mix, looked kind of like old Huxley here, at least that's how I remember him looking anyway. He had a white spot on his forehead right here." Ellie pointed to the center of Hux's forehead just above his eyes. "So I named him Star."

Charlotte smiled. "Cute."

"I took him home and Jack told me to get rid of him. He hated dogs, which isn't too surprising since he seemed to hate damn near everything other than drinking and beating his wife. I went out into the woods and made a little spot for Star, hoping he'd stay, hoping I could keep him a secret. I took the pillow from my bed and some blankets and scrap wood and built this sad little shelter for him. My plan worked for about a week, but then I woke up one morning to old Jack shouting my name outside, interlaced with a string of creative profanity, of course. I went out and both my mom and him were there, old Jack was absolutely fuming. He had a shovel in one hand and a half-empty bottle of Kentucky Choice in the other. When he saw me come out, he looked at me with bloodshot eyes and said, 'You little cunt, I told you to get rid of that mutt.' He pointed toward the woods with his whiskey bottle still in hand. I saw Star pacing back and forth at the edge of our property, scared and confused. Then Jack said, 'If you can't handle it, then you're gonna watch the way I handle it,' and he made this ridiculous gesture with the shovel over his head, like he was a Spartan about to go into battle and the shovel was his spear."

Charlotte put a hand to her mouth. "Oh my god, did he hurt the dog?"

Ellie let her fingers run through Hux's fur and watched

the scene play out in her head as she described it. "My mother put a hand on his shoulder, I think she was trying to calm him down, but he just shoved her off, and as he did, he dropped the bottle of Kentucky Choice. That set him off like a volcano. He started screaming, 'Look what you did!' He grabbed my mother's arm at the wrist and twisted it. Her arm bent at a crazy angle as the bones broke, and I heard this god-awful sickening snap. I swear I can still hear it replaying in my head just like the day it happened. Then my mother screamed and started to sob and babble apologies. Old Jack just held her wrist at that awful angle in a way no arm should bend. It looked fake, like her arm was made of rubber. He just kept saying the same thing over and over. 'Look what you did! Look what you did!' He finally let go of her wrist and she dropped to her knees and cradled her arm to her chest, but he wasn't finished yet. He grabbed the hair on the back of her head and slapped her face a few times, and then forced her head down into the puddle of whiskey like she was a dog who had peed on the floor. All the time chanting, 'Look what you did!'

"I didn't even see him coming, but out of nowhere Star latched onto Jack's arm and started to shake and growl. Old Jack let out a scream like I've never heard since. The scream of a man who loved to give pain but had no concept of how it felt. Here he was finally getting a little taste of his own work. My mother sat up, she was screaming and lying in the dirt, cradling her shattered arm. Her mouth and cheeks were caked in whiskey-soaked mud, blood ran from her nose and dripped onto her white blouse, it ran down the cloth like... little fingers. Red tendrils clawing across white. Jack was screaming and trying to pry Star off his arm, and Star just shook his head side to side as his teeth ripped deeper into flesh. Finally, he kicked Star in the ribs and got him to let go."

Ellie paused and looked intently at Hux. The dog rested peacefully upon her lap as she brushed her hand through his fur. "Finally, it was my turn to scream. Old Jack brought down the shovel. Star yelped and scurried backward, but it was too late. Jack brought the shovel down again and again. Then, when he was satisfied, he looked at me with a wild hate in his eyes that I'd never seen before or since. His left arm was soaked in blood, and I could see tendons and muscle where Star had ripped the skin clean off. In his right hand he held the shovel, caked in blood and chunks of flesh. I stopped screaming, and I ran."

Charlotte still held a hand over her mouth, and two tear tracks ran down either side of her face. "What did you do? Did he catch you?"

Ellie shook her head and fought against the tears that demanded to come. She gripped Hux even tighter. She felt his warmth and smelled the musk of his fur. "He didn't catch me. I don't know if he even chased me, to be honest, or if he was too preoccupied with himself. I never went back to that trailer. I stayed with friends for a few nights and eventually I got in touch with my aunt and uncle. They were happy to take me in, to take me away from that place, away from him. Neither of my parents put up a fight. Jack was probably glad to see me go, and I think after what happened that day, my mother understood that it was what was best for me.

"I only saw my father one more time before he died. It was after my mother's funeral. I decided I was going to tell him to his face what a worthless piece of shit he was. I had this whole speech planned out with some great lines, words I'd thought about a hundred times over. Then when I saw him there, all I saw was a weak and pathetic old man. He was alone and hated by everyone, no love in his life, no future. I knew he would sit alone in that trailer day after day with *nothing*. That was enough for me. Seeing him for how small he really was, it was better than any words I could've spoken."

"I'm so glad you got out of there, but I really feel for your mom," Charlotte said.

Ellie nodded. "Me too. For years I wanted to come back for her, but she passed away while I was in college before I had the means to do anything. I guess that regret could be part of why I've been dreaming about her."

"And poor Star too, my god."

"I dream about him sometimes too, but only ever good dreams. He never knew it, but he saved me that day. He got me away from that place." Ellie scratched Hux behind the ears.

Charlotte took Ellie's hand in hers. "I think maybe he did know it."

Heavy footsteps crossed the floor above them, nearly stomping. A door slammed shut.

"Must be Alaina I guess?" Charlotte said.

"What is she doing up there, moving furniture?"

Charlotte snorted. "Maybe I'll go up and check on her. She wanted to be alone, but after everything that's happened today, I'll feel better knowing she's all right." She gathered the laptop and headphones, then stopped on the way out.

"Speaking of dreams, I'm praying for pleasant ones tonight, I hope yours are the same."

"Me too."

Ellie heard the steps creak as Charlotte made her way up the staircase to the second floor. She stroked a hand through Hux's fur and listened as the rain outside let up, until all that remained was a soft drizzle as the setting sun peeked between the clouds.

"Ellie! Ellie, where are you?" Charlotte yelled as she raced down the stairs. At the clatter of her footsteps and panic in her voice, Hux's eyes jolted open and he exploded off Ellie's lap toward the dining room door.

Charlotte stopped in the doorway and Hux greeted her, curious about the sudden commotion. Eyes wide and out of breath, Charlotte exclaimed, "Oh thank god!"

Ellie shrugged. "What's wrong?"

"I can't find Alaina, I was worried you'd be gone too!" Charlotte said between heavy breaths.

"What do you mean you can't find her?"

Charlotte calmed herself and breathed deep before she continued. "I looked for her where we heard the footsteps, the bedroom above us, but she wasn't there. I checked her room and the monitoring station after that, but they were both empty too. Then I checked the rest of the bedrooms. I called her name in each one, but she just wasn't in any of them! She's gone."

CHAPTER 13

"S he must be downstairs or outside," Ellie said.

"No, I went upstairs right after we heard her! She couldn't have come down. I think..." Charlotte looked over her shoulder as if something might have been lurking behind her. She spoke barely above a whisper. "What if the house took her?"

"Charlotte, come on."

"I know you don't believe, but she's gone! Look. Alaina! Alaina!" Charlotte cupped her hands around her mouth and yelled at the top of her lungs. The sound of her voice echoed in the hall and throughout the old house. There was no response.

Thoughts rushed through Ellie's head, and she tried to distill them into something coherent. Charlotte was right, the stairs in the entrance hall were the only way between the first and second floor, that they knew of at least. It was unlikely Alaina managed to sneak by Charlotte and make it downstairs. "Did you check the cameras?" she asked.

Charlotte shook her head, then yelled for Alaina again. "Alaina! Can you hear me?" The shouting riled up Hux, and he barked in response.

"Hux, no!" Ellie walked to the archway where Charlotte stood, and placed her hands gently onto Charlotte's shoulders. "Calm down, we'll figure this out. Why don't you take a look at the cameras while I check the rooms down here just in case?"

"I don't think we should split up," Charlotte said. Tears began to well in the corners of her eyes. "I don't want to be alone. Will you please come with me? We can check the cameras together and then check the rooms together."

Ellie nodded. "We can do that. We'll search together. The three of us."

The women made their way upstairs while Hux followed at their heels. The monitoring station was empty, just as Charlotte said, and eerily quiet as well. The silence was broken only by the steady whir of laptop fans. Charlotte sat before the bank of monitors and opened the folder of archived videos. She fast forwarded through the cameras one-by-one, watching the events of the afternoon play out.

"That settles it then, she didn't come downstairs," Ellie said. "Unless she crawled out a window, she has to be up here still."

Charlotte spun the office chair around to face Ellie. "God, I hope you're right about the paranormal, because this feels wrong to me, Ellie. I'm not sure I want to be in this house anymore."

Ellie sighed. "Let's go through all the rooms one by one,

this time we'll have three pairs of eyes and a really good nose searching. Did you check the attic?"

Charlotte shook her head. "Why would she be up there?"

"I don't know, but we need to check. That's where we'll start. We'll go top to bottom."

Hux followed the women as they searched the attic and the entire second floor, calling Alaina's name every step of the way. They checked each bedroom, bathroom, and closet, including the one in Julie's room that had been wallpapered off. They looked inside wardrobes and under beds. Every window was shut and locked. In Alaina's guest room, her clothes, bags, and belongings were untouched. Ellie opened Alaina's chest of prized trinkets and unwrapped the book buried beneath red and green cloth.

"What's that?" Charlotte asked.

"One of Alaina's books, she called it *The Wheel*." Ellie rewrapped the leather-bound tome and gently returned it to the trunk. "Alaina wouldn't have left Bruker House without it, not voluntarily at least."

"She isn't here," Charlotte said. Her voice trembled, and the volume she spoke at was probably a little louder than she intended. "She's just gone. Disappeared like the others. The house took her."

Ellie shook her head. "No, we need to check downstairs still, and the cellar."

"She wasn't on the cameras! She didn't even come down the stairs!"

Ellie kept herself calm and collected. It was a shield, a protection against the acceptance of Charlotte's claim, acceptance of the supernatural. "What if there's another way? A servant's staircase, or a hidden passage. We found one hidden room already, why couldn't there be more? We just don't know."

"That doesn't make any sense. We just checked the entire floor, there's no way down. We've been calling her name!"

"She could be outside and didn't hear us. The cameras could have glitched and not caught her going out for a walk. There are a thousand possibilities." Deep down, Ellie knew how the words sounded. She knew she was grasping, but she *had* to grasp.

Charlotte shook her head. "Ellie, there's no way. She's gone."

Ellie put a hand on Charlotte's shoulder. "Search the downstairs with me, she could be unconscious or hurt, we can't leave it open-ended."

Charlotte looked at the floor and nodded in reluctance. "Okay. We'll check the rest of the house."

They searched room by room and opened every pantry and closet on the first floor. They inspected every dark corner of the cold and musty cellar, between construction supplies, towers of boxes and furniture, and in the small cave. They called Alaina's name as they went, but they were answered with silence.

Charlotte and Ellie stepped onto Bruker House's front porch. The rain had subsided, but moisture still hung heavy in the evening air. The smell of wet earth flowed from the misty forest. In the west, a sliver of orange glow was still visible as the sun tucked beneath the horizon and yielded its domain to the moon. Charlotte called far and loud for Alaina. There was no response. The Wagoneer stood alone by the gate, the only means they had to stray very far from the house.

"The house took her just like it took all the others," Charlotte said. Her face was painted with fear.

"I don't believe that. I refuse to believe that. Let's check the second floor again and we'll be extra thorough."

"No! I won't go back in there, and I don't think you should either." Charlotte stepped away from the house and down the porch steps. "Let's drive back into town and get help. We can even call David."

"We'd be leaving Alaina here by herself. She didn't respond; she could be hurt or unconscious just like Lou. We can't just leave her here."

Charlotte took Ellie's hands in hers and looked directly into her eyes. She was several inches taller than Ellie, and for the first time since they met Ellie noticed how imposing she could be. "Look at me, cher. She's gone. We looked everywhere. We called her name. We know what happens to people at Bruker House. It really does take people, it isn't just a myth. She's gone just like all the others."

Ellie pulled her hands away from Charlotte. "No, that just isn't how things work. I didn't believe that the disappearances were supernatural when I first heard about them, and I still don't believe it now. The best explanation is always the simplest, and that means something physical is happening here, not magic. We're missing something in that house. Alaina is stuck there and maybe hurt. For Christ's sake, we heard her walking across the floor above us not five minutes before you went up there!"

Charlotte's eye widened. "That wasn't her, and you know it."

"No, I don't know it actually. Tell me, who else would it be?"

"Ellie, come on."

"I won't leave."

"Ellie, please!" Charlotte begged. She took Ellie's hands again. "Come back to town with me, we'll get help. You don't have to prove anything, I'm perfectly willing to admit that there's a rational explanation for everything, but we can't do this by ourselves. Don't go back in there."

Ellie pulled a hand out of Charlotte's grip and reached into her pocket. She pulled out the keys to the Wagoneer and handed them over. "Here. Take the Wagoneer into town and get help. I'll stay behind and look for Alaina."

Charlotte tried to hand the keys back. "No, cher, I'm not leaving you here."

"You said it yourself. There's a physical explanation for everything happening, but we still need help. So, I'll wait here while you get help."

"You can't stay alone in this place!"

"I won't be alone, I'll have Hux with me." Ellie bent down and stroked Hux's back.

"No, cher." Charlotte tried to hand the keys back again, but Ellie refused to take them.

Ellie took a step back from Charlotte toward the house. "Then come back inside with me and help me look."

Charlotte gazed up at the house, and a deep frown formed on her face. What had been a mixture of concern and fear transformed into pure unadulterated terror as she took in the sight before her. Charlotte shook her head slowly. "I can't. I can't go back in. Alaina was right, we should never have come here. We're playing with something we shouldn't be. This place is a lion's den."

"Then go back to town and get us some help. I won't be alone, Hux will keep me safe. Hell, with any kind of luck, I'll find Alaina." Ellie stayed calm, collected, and rational. It kept the world in control. If she slipped and admitted what was happening here was strange, maybe even impossible, that's when it would all come crashing down. Like Atlas, she held the rational world atop her shoulders, lest it collapse into chaos.

"Ellie, you don't have anything to prove. You can come with me, and no one will think it's because you thought this place was haunted."

"I'm not trying to prove anything. I'm staying in case Alaina turns up and needs help."

"Please, cher." Tears ran down Charlotte's cheek. She clasped her hands together as if in prayer. The Wagoneer keys dangled loosely from one finger, and Aunt Shirley's pink rabbit's foot charm swayed back and forth from it. "Please come back to town with me. I'm scared, I'll admit to that. I don't want to go alone, and I really don't want you to stay." The last words were punctuated by several sobs. "I want to believe Alaina is okay, but she's gone, just like the others. She's gone without a trace. We'll bring the police up here to search in the morning, but they won't find anything, just like they never found anything before." The sobs came heavier and more frequent. "And I'm afraid that if you stay, you'll be gone too."

Ellie paused to think at the end of Charlotte's plea, but the pause was only a gesture for Charlotte's benefit. She had already made up her mind. "I'm staying, Charlotte. I'm sorry." Ellie turned and walked toward the double front doors of Bruker House. Hux hesitated for only a moment, then followed behind her.

"Cher... Ellie," Charlotte said. Her voice cracked with emotion.

Ellie didn't turn around. She stepped through the doors and shut them behind her. She watched through the front window as Charlotte started the Wagoneer and drove it through the muddy courtyard, then through the front gate. The glow of the Jeep's headlights grew dim and faded into darkness as Charlotte made her way down the dark forest road back to town.

CHAPTER 14

E llie gazed out into the cold night long after the last flash of the Wagoneer's lights dipped behind the trees. She wondered if Charlotte would be safe on the muddy road through the dark and misty forest. She thought about her isolation, in the wilderness without a means of transportation, or even a way to call for help. Above all else, she considered the house. Despite her claim that there was nothing supernatural and nothing to fear from this place, a feeling deep within her gut regretted the decision to stay. There was a strange smell in the foyer, rotten and sour. There was a silence in the house, deafening quiet. Bruker House felt like a corpse beginning to fester.

Ellie wasn't alone though. She looked down at Hux by her side. He waited expectantly, ready to follow her wherever they would go. She bent and ruffled his fur, and he responded with several attempts to lick her face.

She glanced back toward the gate and to the winding road down the hill. In the distance she saw a light. At first, she thought it was the Wagoneer's headlights, maybe the road was impassable and Charlotte had decided to return, but the direction was wrong. The Wagoneer's taillights had disappeared to the south; this new light was in the west, not from the direction of the road, but from within the forest. It didn't burn bright white like a headlamp, but a warm orange, flickering like a flame. It reminded Ellie of an oil lamp, the kind an old-timey miner might carry as he delved deep into the earth.

It was the same light she'd seen from her window on her first night at Bruker House. Lou had called it a will-o'-the-wisp, a fool's flame; follow it and be doomed to lose your way in the forest and the bogs. Ellie didn't buy into the superstition about ghost lights, but there was something out there, something aglow in the night. A building, a person, maybe even Alaina.

In the front hall, Ellie opened one of Charlotte's pelican cases. She sifted through trail cams and boxes of batteries until she landed on what she was searching for: a flashlight. She stepped into the crisp evening air that hung heavy over the grounds of Bruker House. The creeping cold nipped at Ellie's face, and she could see her breath as it condensed into the cool night. It was colder now that Charlotte was gone. Clouds and fog blotted out the stars and moon, the sky was a pitch-black void. There was not one speck of light outside Bruker House save for the dancing orange flame beyond the tree line.

"Alaina! Are you out there?" Ellie called. She waited for a response, but there was none. The only sound from the forest was the patter of water droplets as they fell from tree branches onto wet leaves below. Ellie switched on the flashlight and pointed it into the forest. "Alaina? Who's out there?" she shouted. She swept the beam across the trees, but the flickering orange flame was beyond the flashlight's reach.

Hux stared in the direction of the light and gave a long quiet whine like a tea kettle.

"I'm coming out there, and I have a dog with me!" Ellie was aware of how weak the threat sounded, but some part of her still thought there might be a person, or even persons, behind the disappearances. She didn't like the explanation, and she liked the thought of someone silently watching her from the between the trees even less, but at least it was a *real* explanation; it wasn't magic.

Ellie stepped off the porch and walked toward the light, Hux following at her heels. They walked past the collapsing carriage house and into the trees. Wet leaves made sloppy sounds beneath Ellie's boots as they trudged through the forest. The flashlight lit up the trees directly in front of her, but her world was small, shrunk down to a ten-foot-wide field of view within the narrow beam. She looked back toward Bruker House. In a flash of panic, she thought that it might not be there, that she had followed the light deep into the forest and become lost like a fool from Lou's myth. Yet there it stood. Amber light burned in its windows like watchful eyes, the house looked enormous as it wallowed in its throne upon the hill. She wrapped her arms around her midsection and pulled her jacket close to her body as the night grew ever colder. She walked on toward the orange glow.

Ellie's light landed on the source. Tucked away in the side of a small berm was a crevice lined with stacked stone.

The opening was no more than five feet tall and barely a foot wide, and branches and roots from the surrounding trees masked its entrance, but in the dark of night the orange light from within marked its location like a spot lamp.

She recognized the crack in the hillside immediately— little Julie stood beside it in one of the Campbell family photos. Ellie's heart thumped in her chest at the thought of who or what she might find inside.

"Alaina, are you in there?" Ellie meant to call into the entrance, but her voice came out just above a whisper. As a meek addendum, she added, "Anyone?" She waited, and dreaded a response.

Ellie turned to look at Bruker House once more; still there, it loomed above the forest, watching, waiting. She pointed the flashlight down at Hux by her side, the pupils of his eyes flashed green and contracted as he stared back into the light. Mist puffed from his nostrils into the flashlight's beam, then vanished into the darkness. "Don't you dare leave my side," Ellie said. She knew the words weren't needed, because both of them understood their arrangement. He would be there for her without question, always.

Ellie took a deep breath, then entered the passage. She ducked her head and contorted her body to squeeze through the tight opening. A familiar smell of wet earth filled her nostrils. The crooked walls of the tight passage were rough-hewn from stone, the ground was flooded with ice cold water that rose halfway up the side of her boots. Although she thought it impossible, she had dreamt of this place. Adrenaline flooded her veins as she anticipated what might await her at the end of the tunnel.

There was the domed cavern from her dream. The candles and symbols that decorated its walls were long gone, in their place lay bare stone and the remnants of ancient wax. The stone slab in the center was devoid of corpses, but on it burned a single white candle beside a leather-bound book. Ellie's breath grew heavy, her heart pounded in her chest, her feet ached in the icy water. She took a step forward into the stacked stone cavern and panned the flashlight beam across the walls. On the ceiling, carved deep into the rock, was the same symbol they found hidden in a Bruker House closet. The bizarre geometry twisted in confusing knots, lines folded into themselves along paths that seemed to defy logic. A feeling rose up in the pit of Ellie's stomach that screamed for her to leave, that told her she wasn't meant to be in this place.

Hux sloshed through the flooded floor and lapped at the muddy water, unconcerned with prophetic dreams, ghost lights, or bizarre necrophilic rituals.

Ellie opened the book, and the candle's flame flickered as a breeze passed through the cavern. A tingle of fear ran down her spine. Inside the book were lines of handwritten foreign text, geometric patterns, and sketches of rituals. The ink of the page swayed in the light of the candle. Ellie wondered if the book might belong to Alaina, if she had been in the cavern, if it was her who had lit the candle. She scanned page after page of strange symbols until she landed on a note nestled between two of them. There, in large flowing script, read, *To my beloved Helena, I finally found what we've been looking for, A.B.* The diagram on the page depicted a corpse on a slab. A series of symbols were drawn below—a spiral, a stylized triangle, a star, a crescent.

As Ellie read the page, the candle flame fluttered and extinguished. Paraffin particles spiraled upward in the beam of the flashlight while terror exploded within Ellie. She panicked. She ran to the exit and squeezed through the tight passage, stones and roots scraped against her as she scrambled to escape. She tripped over a rock, stumbled out into the cold wet night, then spun around and pointed the flashlight beam at the passage, waiting for what might follow from the darkness.

The flashlight shook in Ellie's hand as she watched for what felt like hours. Nothing came. She caught her breath and looked at Hux by her side. "It's just a candle," she said between breaths. The cold night air scratched in her throat. "But who lit it?"

Bruker House stood tall in the distance, a black silhouette marked by burning amber windows. A blue-white corona glowed around its edge as moonlight broke through the thick blanket of clouds. The house looked powerful, like a ruler gazing across the vast stretches of their kingdom. It was a castle. A bastion of safety against the cold and unknown wilds of the forest. Despite its odd smell, disturbing silence, and unsavory reputation, Bruker House promised light, warmth, and comfort within its walls.

Ellie trekked back to the house. Her boots sunk deep into mud and leaves with each step, her flashlight panned back and forth in search of unwelcome surprises, and perhaps to ward them off. Amidst the steady drip of water from the tree-tops, a bird sang. Ellie recognized the call from Charlotte's trail cam video.

It was a whippoorwill.

THE SMELL HIT Ellie like a semi-truck the instant she opened the front door. Something was rotten within the walls of Bruker House. She retched and raised a hand to cover her mouth and nose; it was all she could do to soften the scent of decay. When Ellie was a child, a rat had died inside the walls of their trailer. For weeks it stank of rotting flesh until her father finally cut a hole in the paneling to remove the rodent remains. Now Bruker House, too, reeked of concentrated death. Something primal within her screamed to leave the house, but the temperature outside was dropping rapidly and the promise of warmth within the house's walls outweighed her instinct to leave.

Hux waited just outside the double doors. The dog who usually insisted on darting through any open crack now stood just outside with no desire to enter.

"Come on, bud." Ellie crouched down and beckoned Hux inside. After the initial impact of the smell, its intensity subsided, or at least temporarily abated its assault. Each new breath inside the house was semi-tolerable.

Hux whined and took two steps back from the doorway. A sickening tingle grew in the pit of Ellie's stomach, it twisted and writhed as tendrils of fear spread through her extremities. She turned around to face the large and imposing entrance hall. The vacant space was enormous; she felt like an insect trapped under glass. She turned back toward the open doorway and to Hux, who waited for her to join him outside.

"Huxley." She said his name as warm and gentle as she could. "Come."

Hux sniffed the air, then cautiously stepped through the doorway into the house. He sneezed and snuffled as he crossed the threshold.

Ellie ruffled the dog's head. "I know it's stinky, but I need you with me, bud." She took one last look at the world outside Bruker House. Without the orange glow, the forest was a black hole. She pushed the double doors shut with a heavy thud.

Hux stared up at her and panted. It was too cold for him to be overheated; the panting was a signal of anxiety and stress. She slid Charlotte's flashlight into the back pocket of her jeans, then took Hux's head in her hands. "Maybe we should see where that smell is coming from, huh? Could be something left out in the kitchen."

Ellie crossed the entrance hall and opened the door to the dining room. She switched on the lights and gasped as they revealed a crimson nightmare. The room bled like an open wound. The red stain had grown to consume the entire ceiling, its bloody fingers reaching down the walls and clawing at the floor.

Ellie threw a hand to her mouth. "The hell?" she muttered to herself. She remembered the afternoon rain and convinced herself the roof must leak. Rainwater ran down a wall and pooled on the dining room ceiling. No ghosts or fairies, just a simple leak.

The kitchen was spotless. There was no food left out. No strange smells from the garbage or the sink, at least not so far as Ellie could tell. By now she was noseblind to the odor that permeated the house. She made her peace with it; there were more pressing mysteries to solve.

Ellie lay in the parlor and stared up at the coffered ceiling, pure white without a hint of red. She thought about the unresolved mysteries. Some were hardly a mystery at all. Lou collapsed, but he was very old with a known heart condition. There was a red stain in the dining room, but water stains are common. The cameras caught a shadow in the parlor, but she reproduced it with a flickering light, and old lighting sometimes flickers.

Other mysteries were harder to accept. Who lit the candle in the cavern and left the book behind? Why did the house reek? Above all else, where was Alaina? *Strange things are afoot at the Circle K*, she thought. Bill and Ted would be inclined to agree. There was one thing she was certain about: Charlotte had been right, she was trying to prove something by staying here.

A dull thump sounded upstairs, and a wave of panic rushed through Ellie. Heavy footsteps crossed the floor above her, hard-soled boots against a wooden floor. Every footfall hit her in the chest like a hammer. Her breathing intensified and she poured everything she had into keeping still and quiet. For the first time since she was a child, Ellie felt absolute abject terror.

Hux stared at the ceiling with his ears pinned back and let out a low growl.

"Shhh," Ellie whispered softly. She placed her hand on Hux's head to calm him.

The footsteps stopped, and a door slammed shut.

Ellie would have given anything to have the Wagoneer

parked outside again. Keys in her hand, pink rabbit's foot dangling, thirty feet away from escape, and a lifetime of ignorance of whoever or whatever crossed the floor upstairs.

For what seemed like hours, Ellie remained perfectly still, waiting, listening. All the moisture had left her mouth, but she managed to whisper one word, hardly more than a puff of air. "Alaina?" There was no response, not that anyone farther than five feet away could have heard her call.

She sat up on the sofa and mustered the strength to call out again. "Alaina!" This time loud enough to echo through the hall. She waited for a response, but none came.

She breathed deep and built the confidence to call out a third time. "Alaina, if that's you up there, you need to say something. If anyone else is up there, I'm coming up with my dog."

No response.

Ellie looked to Hux and he looked back at her, waiting for her to take the lead. She looked around the room for a weapon. A pewter candlestick rested on a stand beside the sofa. She picked it up and felt the weight of the makeshift cudgel in her right hand. It would do. She remembered Charlotte's Clue reference, only instead of Colonel Mustard in the library, it would be Professor Hawthorne in the bedroom.

Ellie stepped into the entrance hall, now larger and more foreboding than ever. The brass chandelier hung like a deadly trap that dared her to walk beneath it. The once beautiful grand staircase twisted at an unnatural angle like a broken spine. The upstairs hallway was a gaping maw which opened into a sick strange darkness beyond. Ellie's eyes darted back and forth between every unseen corner and shad-owed nook as she felt a newfound appreciation for agoraphobia.

"We're coming up now," Ellie called out as she and Hux climbed the staircase. The treads creaked and groaned with each step, announcing their ascent. Ellie wiped her sweaty palms dry on her pants and adjusted her grip on the candle-stick as she crested the top of the steps.

The second floor was quiet and empty.

"Who's up here?" she yelled. Adrenaline gave her strength, but caused her voice to quiver, broadcasting her fear to whoever might be listening.

Ellie walked to the end of the hall, to the bedroom that sat above the parlor. Julie's old room with hideous yellow and green floral print wallpaper. She held the candlestick ready to swing at whatever she might find behind the door and pushed it open. Empty. The closet door lay open, the space beyond the threshold black as night. Ellie felt sick at the thought of what might lay in wait on the other side.

"I know you're in there, come out now!" Ellie said with as much confidence as she could manage. She held the candle-stick with one hand, with the other she retrieved Charlotte's flashlight from the back pocket of her jeans. She clicked the light on and directed the beam through the open closet door. She checked behind her once, then crept toward the closet with the candlestick held high, her heart heavy in her chest. The closet was empty.

Ellie's relief was short-lived, as the flashlight's beam landed on the strange symbol carved into the far wall. Streaks of red liquid wept from the recesses of the shape, and ran down the wood-paneled wall in crimson trails, disappearing between gaps in the floorboards.

"It's just resin," Ellie said to Hux, as if he were the one who needed to be convinced of an explanation for the seeping fluid. "Maybe water from the rain affected the wood."

Ellie turned her attention back to the footsteps. Whoever or whatever walked across the floor was gone, but to where? And how did they get there?

Ellie left the bedroom and checked around every corner as she made her way across the upstairs hallway to the monitoring station. From there she could watch the house from multiple points of view. Inside, the bank of computer monitors displayed black-and-white video feeds from around the house. Laptop fans whirred and LEDs flashed on and off. As Ellie sat at the desk, she heard a door unlatch from behind. She spun around in the chair and listened while Hux lowered his head and let out a deep growl. From the hall, a door hinge whined as it slowly creeped open and culminated in several distinctive staccato pops as it slowed to a stop. Ellie peaked around the edge of the monitoring station doorway. At the end of the hall, the attic door stood open, witches stairs leading into darkness above.

CHAPTER 15

A cold draft streamed from the attic and poured down the staircase like an icy river. The first few steps of the witches stairs were visible, then obscured into darkness as they ascended into the pitch-black attic above. Ellie stood in the open doorway and clicked on the flashlight. A cool blue beam spread across the steps, up through the rectangular opening at their terminus, and finally landed on the rafters beyond. She was reminded of Thomas Huxley, *Follow humbly wherever and to whatever abyss nature leads.* Here before her was an abyss, and she had no desire to follow it.

"Alaina?" Ellie called up the stairs. The name came out quiet. She looked down at Hux by her side and found the strength to call again. "Alaina!" she shouted. "Alaina, are you up there?" She paused and listened for a response. None came.

Ellie wiped off her sweaty palms and tightened her grip on the candlestick, then began her ascent into the attic. Partway up the stairs, Hux whimpered from behind. She turned back to see his silhouette, pure black against the light of the hallway beyond. "I know you struggle with these stairs, bud. Can't you do it? Just for me?"

Hux whined and placed his front feet on the first step; it was as far as he would go.

"You stay down there and watch my back then." For the first time since she entered Bruker House, Ellie walked alone.

She crested the top of the stairs and swept the flashlight beam across the attic. A crisscrossing framework of joists and rafters cast a tangled web of shadows across the underside of the roof.

"Alaina?" Ellie called. A light breeze howled through gaps in the drafty old walls; it was the only sound to break the silence. She looked back down the stairs to see Hux waiting patiently at their base.

Ellie panned the flashlight slowly across each wall. It landed on nothing but dusty wood and spiderwebs. She walked around two crumbling chimney stacks that blocked her field of view. A geometric web of shadows moved along with her, desperately clinging to the darkness in every nook and corner.

Shadows and dust; the attic was empty. Ellie told herself the attic door probably didn't latch after she and Charlotte searched for Alaina. It was a drafty old house, and a light breeze had pushed the door open. She had let herself get sucked into the mythology of this house and now here she was, jumping at shadows.

She made her way to descend the staircase when a cold chill swept over her. She turned and gave the attic one last look. As she swept the flashlight's beam, she noticed a dark corner on the opposite wall. The web of shadows culminated there. The flashlight illuminated the entire opposite wall, save for the one dark spot. The corner was disturbingly dark, endlessly dark. She moved the flashlight away and then back again and watched as the shadows moved along with the light, all except the one corner that remained a pitch-black void. She stared into the dark abyss and a sick tingle of fear bloomed in the pit of her stomach.

Hux whined from the bottom of the stairs.

She gazed into the void, hypnotized by its dark and impenetrable depth. It stared right back at her. Her stomach sank deeper, and tears welled in her eyes. She was small and powerless, a little girl back in Missouri again, alone and afraid.

A voice in Ellie's head pled for reason. It insisted she was being silly, there was nothing to be afraid of in that corner, it was just dark. It was silly for her to be so frightened, irrational even, and what greater sin was there for a scientist and a skeptic than to be irrational? She hadn't seen or heard any danger. She could probably reach out and touch that corner, and she wouldn't feel any danger either. Alaina's words echoed in her head; she was a blind man who refused to believe that a lion existed until she reached out and touched one.

Alaina was wrong. Ellie wouldn't reach out and touch it, because she felt something, something less tangible than her other senses but equally as important. It was an ancient feeling, older than humanity. It said, *There's something in here with you, something in that void, and if you don't get out of here right now, you're going to be dead.* That same feeling had risen to the surface in countless humans before her, and the ones who heeded it had survived to pass it on generation after generation. Ellie knew she would be wise to heed its warning now.

She took a step back toward the attic staircase. "Hux?" Her voice choked with fear and what came out was more of a whimper than a word.

From the floor below, Hux let out low growl, a warning deep and long. Ancient senses arose within him too, but without the burden of logic or doubt. A visceral voice called from his ancestors with a simple message: *Kill or be killed.*

Ellie took another step back toward the stairs, but her focus never turned from the void. When she was at the top of the stairs, the impenetrable darkness shifted and grew. Any remaining doubt Ellie had of its danger was shattered. She stood frozen, petrified by shock and fear. She stared in disbelief as the void twisted and bent into unnatural shapes. It emitted a low pulsating drone, an ethereal hum, as it expanded from a small spot in the corner into a mass that consumed the entire wall. The beam of Ellie's flashlight faded into obscurity as it shone into the inky black abyss.

Hux barked from the floor below in a steady rhythm peppered with whimpers and snarls.

The void swirled and grew, and at its center, a vague humanoid shape took form. Ellie recognized the silhouette immediately. Jack Hawthorne stood in the center of the void and stared at her, stared *through* her. Helena Bruker's voice sounded, *They all died screaming, you'll die screaming too.* Her father raised his right arm toward her and carrion black tendrils grew from his fingertips; they twisted and writhed in her direction. Ellie's feet finally found the strength to move. She hurled the pewter candlestick at the twisted shape and ran down the attic stairs, struggling not to stumble on the awkward steps. From behind she heard a guttural inhuman scream.

Hux's silhouette was at the bottom of the staircase barking and snarling. As she made it halfway down the steps, he turned and ran down the hall. "Hux, wait!" Ellie yelled. He bolted down the corridor and rounded the corner before she could get more words out.

A second unholy scream rose behind Ellie as she reached the bottom of the attic staircase. The otherworldly sound held power, there was a palpable violence and depth to it. The tone penetrated to Ellie's core like a concert bass. Bruker House shook in harmony with the preternatural screech, and the hall around her darkened.

She dared a glance over her shoulder. The doorway to the attic was gone, in its place was a black abyss. At the center stood her father, and Helena Bruker, and countless others folded into one incomprehensible shape, and it was much closer than she'd hoped.

Inky tendrils grew from the presence and felt along the walls and ceiling. They reached for her, curling and snapping like bullwhips as she ran through a hallway that now felt a thousand miles long. She felt something cold wrap around her ankle, and she collapsed to the floor. The flashlight fell from her hand and put on a brief light show as it spun across the hallway runner and came to rest against the wall. Ellie hit the floor with a grunt and screamed out as the freezing cold tendril gripped her ankle like a vise. She tried to pull away, but it yanked her back and climbed farther up her leg. The pain from its icy grip was excruciating, and Ellie felt the warmth of her body drain against the relentless cold.

The deep throbbing drone grew ever louder as the void inched forward. Ellie struggled to free her leg from the tendril's grasp while several others wrapped around her arms and pulled her back toward the attic. The hallway, the house, and reality itself lurched. The walls and ceiling shifted back and forth between plaster and a vast stygian black sky, a starless expanse yawning into eternity. The floor faded between oak planks and an alien desert with a horizon that stretched beyond comprehension. All around Ellie, strange geometries flexed and morphed in one moment, then settled back into garish wallpaper patterns the next. She was slipping. The presence before her—demon, spirit, ancient god, whatever the thing may be—wasn't just pulling her across the hallway floor, it was pulling her from this reality into its own.

Ellie caught movement from the corner of her eye. Not a strange otherworldly shape, but a familiar one. Hux sprinted past her, his body low to the ground. His claws dug into an oriental carpet in one moment, and into endless desert the next. His ears were pinned tight against his head and his lips pulled back to reveal dozens of bared teeth. He was a blur as he ran at full speed toward the presence. He leapt from a surface that simultaneously belonged to both a Victorian house and some distant world. Hux flew through the air with his mouth open wide, and his powerful jaws clamped onto the humanoid shape in the center of the void. His teeth sank deep into its throat, and a chorus of ten thousand voices screamed out in fear and pain that echoed through two realities. Hux hung from his victim's neck, he thrashed his body and dug his claws deep into its chest. Black tendrils whipped and twisted in confusion. Hux pushed his back feet against the presence, and with a savage yank and twist of his head he ripped out the thing's throat and dropped to the ground.

The profane chorus of screams cut short, and only a deep pulsating hum remained. The grip around Ellie's hands and feet loosened, and the inky tendrils retreated as the presence shifted its focus to a newfound threat. Warm air touched Ellie's skin like a soft kiss, and the shifting and merging realities settled into one.

Hux grappled with the creature at the end of the hall. The figure retreated as he barked and snapped at its feet. Oily black tendrils shot at him. He ducked and dodged each attack, too quick for their assault. The two of them were locked in a perverted dance; the void cracked its tendrils at Hux while he snapped powerful jaws in response. It was Hux, though, who was advancing.

Ellie stumbled onto her feet, her limbs felt as though she had run a marathon. "Hux!" she yelled.

The dog ignored her call. He latched onto a tendril that whipped too close to his face. The creature tried to pull back its appendage, but it was too late. Hux held the extremity in an iron grip and shook it violently. The devastating attack ripped the tendril from the rest of the presence, and it flopped onto the ground and dissolved into the floor.

"Hux!" Ellie screamed at the top of her lungs. He snapped out of the frenzy and turned toward Ellie's voice. She beckoned him to come and he ran toward her, leaving his quarry in retreat against the back of the hall.

Ellie and Hux rounded the corner and raced down the grand staircase. The pulsating hum grew into another sickening shriek from above. Bruker House quaked from the base of its foundation to the peak of its tower. The entrance hall chandelier swung back and forth like an elaborate pendulum. A fissure opened in the wall, dust and flecks of plaster rained from the ceiling. Ellie didn't dare look behind her.

She ran across the foyer with Hux close at her heels and threw open the front doors. Hux dashed out first through a dog-sized gap and Ellie trailed behind him. She ran across the muddy courtyard into the cold dark night and didn't look over her shoulder until she was past the front gate. Bruker House stood a thousand feet tall and just as wide, its windows amber eyes ablaze with fire in the dark of night, the double front doors a mouth pinned open in a black and violent scream.

Ellie ran along the forest road until she stumbled and collapsed from exhaustion. Drained of energy by the creature, she couldn't even make it out of sight of the house. Hux laid his head on Ellie's lap as she sat in the dirt heaving the cold midnight air. The world was shrouded in darkness save for Bruker House, which glowed proudly atop its hill.

The night was freezing, and the wet road sapped the heat from Ellie's body. Every breath was razor blades in her throat. She held Hux close to her, but even his warmth wasn't enough to abate the violent shivers that seized her body. The road back to Narramissic was long, and Ellie lacked the strength to stand. She wondered who, come morning, would find her body frozen in the mud.

A deep hum grew. It was coming for her, even out here

the thing from the attic was coming, and Ellie had no strength left to fight it.

The droning hum grew louder yet, but it didn't come from the house, it came from the road ahead. The dark night was bathed in bright light as headlamps broke between the trees, the Wagoneer rounded the corner, and long white beams cut through the forest mist.

Ellie summoned everything she had left within her to stand. She stumbled only once, but caught herself. She raised a hand toward the light and mumbled unintelligible words. Tears poured from her eyes as her savior approached.

The Wagoneer's brakes squealed as it stopped in the road, its engine gently hummed at idle, mist and exhaust swirled around the cab like a spiritual aura. The driver's side door cracked open and Charlotte stepped out. "Ellie? What's—"

Ellie stumbled toward the Wagoneer and managed to spit out two sensible words "Drive! Go!" She ripped open the back door; Hux flew in and landed on the bench seat and Ellie followed, clawing her way into the cab. "Drive, just drive," Ellie muttered as she pulled the door shut behind her.

Charlotte threw the Jeep into reverse. After a tight three-point turn, they were driving down the potholed road toward town as fast as they dared.

Ellie watched through the rear window as Bruker House sank farther into the distance. It looked small, just a house on a hill. There was no malicious void, no unholy shrieks, no tendrils bursting from its windows to grab at her. The house looked the same as it did on the day she arrived, but the feelings it provoked within her had changed forever. She knew now the darkness that resided within its walls, the danger that lurked in its depths.

"What happened?" Charlotte asked. Shock and concern were clear in her voice. She glanced in the rearview mirror and Ellie saw her eyes were wide.

Ellie sat in silence, unsure how to even begin to answer the question. She stole another glance through the back window of the Jeep and watched as the amber glow of Bruker House's windows dipped behind a hill, gone from her view. The only sight that remained behind the Wagoneer was a dirt road awash in red light. "It's real. It's all real," Ellie said. She acknowledged the reality of her experience out loud, and the existence of the supernatural was cemented for her.

"What's real? What happened?"

The warm cabin increased Ellie's body temperature enough that she could feel her extremities again. The skin of her arms and legs tingled, and her fingers and toes ached as they welcomed the warmth. "It tried to take me. Whatever it is in that house tried to take me just like the others." She reached for Hux and hugged him close. Tears came in a torrent and ran down her cheeks, landing in his soft fur. "Hux saved me, it's the only way I made it out."

"Oh my god," Charlotte muttered. She raised a few fingers to cover her mouth and checked the rearview mirror to ensure nothing was behind them.

Ellie sobbed against Hux, soaking the dog's fur with tears and snot. He buried his head deep into her chest and accepted the embrace.

Charlotte reached into the back with one hand and placed it gently onto Ellie's knee. "There there, don't cry, cher. Everything'll be okay now. I'll get us a room in town, and you'll come stay the night with me."

The tears didn't completely stop, but Charlotte's touch helped. Ellie settled down and wiped her face with the back of her hand. "I think it got Alaina, I think that's why we couldn't find her."

Charlotte looked at Ellie through the rearview mirror. "You think there's anything we can do? To help her, I mean?"

Ellie shook her head. "I don't know. I just don't know. I saw glimpses of the place that it took her, I don't think anyone can survive there." She sniffled and wiped away more tears. "I don't even know where it is, or *what* it is."

Charlotte rubbed Ellie's knee. "We can't worry about that right now. Let's focus on getting you out of here."

Ellie put her hand atop Charlotte's; it was warm enough to be on fire compared with her own. "Why'd you come back?"

"I was trying to reach David when I had a feeling. Something in me said I needed to face my fear. I needed to go back to Bruker House no matter what I might find there because it was a critical moment in this life. So I went."

Ellie squeezed Charlotte's hand in hers. "Thank god people like you exist."

Charlotte glanced into the rearview mirror and smiled.

Ellie looked back through the rear window again. The forest was quiet. She laughed to herself. "At least Mr. Warwick will be pleased."

"How's that?" Charlotte asked.

"He has my stamp of approval. Bruker House is haunted."

CHAPTER 16

ONE MONTH LATER

Ellie admired the foam of her latte, a stylized swan painted in swirls of white and cashmere. She always felt bad destroying the art, but she took a sip anyway. She cherished the warmth of the hot drink on a cold day. Outside, trees lay bare, birds sang softly, and snowflakes fell, melting as they landed on the pavement. It was Brookhaven's first snow of the year.

Ellie took another sip from her latte and watched shoppers as they marched along Main Street. She spotted David and Charlotte at the crosswalk outside. A bell jingled as they entered the café; she waved and then stood to greet them both

"Hello, cher," Charlotte said. She gave Ellie a warm hug and held the embrace.

David smiled and gave Ellie a nod. "I hope you've been doing well. I see I should've brought my hat, winter's coming early this year." He cocked his head toward the window and the falling snow outside.

"I think we still have a few weeks before it sticks," Ellie said.

"We can only hope." David kept one eye on the flurry outside as he untied his scarf and threw it over the back of a chair.

Ellie returned to her seat and warmed her hands on the mug. "How was the service?"

"It was good, big turnout. A lot of people in this town really loved Lou. You should've come," David said.

"It felt strange, I didn't really know him."

Charlotte unbuttoned her coat. "It was a very religious crowd; I almost skipped it myself because of that. They don't always see eye to eye with my kind, you know."

A waitress stopped at their table and produced a notepad and stubby pencil from the pocket of her apron. "Get you anything?"

"Black coffee," David said.

"Nothing for me thanks," said Charlotte.

The waitress nodded and walked away, notepad unused.

"I'm glad so many people showed up for him. Was there any mention of the house?" Ellie asked.

David shook his head. "No. They said something like, 'He passed while among friends, enjoying one of his many hobbies,' but they didn't mention Bruker House specifically."

Ellie felt a shiver run down her spine as David named the house. She felt cold, like an icy hand held a grip around her core. She took another sip of her latte and focused on its warmth.

"The medical examiner said it was a massive heart attack,

said he was probably gone before I got him back into town," David said.

"I guess we'll never know if the house had anything to do with it," said Charlotte.

David nodded. "And I don't think talking about it at the service would be of any comfort to his grieving family."

Ellie looked between David and Charlotte and tried to judge their thoughts. She spoke quietly, as if they were discussing a secret. "Amongst ourselves though?"

"Well, after what happened to you and Alaina, I wouldn't be surprised if something had come for him too," said Charlotte.

David nodded. "I think that too. I think whatever Ellie saw came for him first, and the shock of it gave him a heart attack. Then later it came for Alaina."

The waitress arrived with a clean mug and an urn of hot coffee. She placed the mug in front of David and poured. The three of them stayed silent as they waited for the waitress to leave.

"Speaking of Alaina, any news from the police investigation?" Charlotte asked.

David took in a deep breath and sighed. "The police organized another search of the grounds two days ago. They didn't find anything. No one wants to give up hope, but we all know about the other disappearances at the house. I don't think they'll find a damned thing."

"What about that cave I told you about?" Ellie asked.

"Yes, an old cellar hole is what they said. They're pretty common across New England."

"Did they find the book?" Ellie asked.

"No, they searched it but they said it was empty."

"So, they didn't find a single clue?" Charlotte asked.

"Nothing. In fact, Alaina isn't the only one who's missing. It turns out a flooring guy who was working on the house is MIA as well. Apparently, he didn't show up for work after we left, so Hank started asking around. No one had seen him in nearly a week. I guess there's no way to know if it was the house or if the guy just ran off. All I know is he worked in the house, and he's also missing." David blew on his coffee and sent swirls of steam across the table.

"The house took two people back to back? Must've been hungry," Charlotte said.

"How are they still doing renovations on that place?" Ellie asked. "After everything that happened? People are missing! Someone died, for Christ's sake!"

David shrugged. "I agree, it's not the decision I would've made, that's for sure. I wrote up a full report of what we found, and I recommended not allowing visitors in the house. Warwick and the others are aware of everything that's happened, but they're moving forward with their plans anyway. The place is set to open in the spring."

Charlotte shook her head. "It's disgusting. They're going to get people killed."

The trio was silent for a moment. Charlotte reached across the table and took Ellie's hand in her own. "How are you holding up, cher?"

Ellie wanted to lie. She wanted to say she'd been doing well, better than last week, but Charlotte deserved the truth. She stared into her mostly empty latte, foam clung to the side of the mug. What had been a swan was now shattered and broken, only fragments remained of the shape that once was. "Not great. I'm still having the nightmares, my father, Bruker House... that thing in the attic. They always end the same way, in that place that it tried to take me. That place haunts me, even during the day. A starless sky arcing above endless desert pavement, a horizon that stretches so far I could walk for ten thousand years and never reach its end, an unrelenting wind that saps every ounce of energy from my body. There is no shelter, no warmth, no future. I wake up screaming half the time, freezing cold and soaked in sweat. Poor Hux is confused and anxious every time, wondering what happened." She played with her mug, spinning it back and forth on its saucer.

Charlotte squeezed her hand. "I'm so sorry, Ellie. I hope it passes with time."

Ellie held back tears. "I just think of Alaina. What if that's where she is? Trapped in that nightmare? My god, I wouldn't wish that on anyone."

"We aren't giving up on her," David said. "The police probably won't find anything, but a few folks from the Society are researching what you described. We'll see what we can find out about it."

"We all have Alaina on our minds and in our hearts, but for now just take care of yourself, cher. The dreams will pass, I know it." Charlotte held her hand tight.

"You know, I've had a few dreams since I got back too. Mostly about that broken window upstairs; it's just there looming over me."

"I didn't notice a broken window," Charlotte said.

"It was right on the front, second story," David said.

Ellie exchanged a glance with Charlotte. She was all but certain there had been no broken windows at Bruker House.

"I know a dream therapist that's worked with a few of us from the Society. I've been thinking about giving him a call. I'll give you his number if you'd like," David said.

Ellie smiled and nodded. "Sure, it's worth a shot I suppose. The lack of sleep is only part of it though. I feel like my entire world has been turned upside down after what happened that night. Things I never thought were possible are suddenly very real."

"Some of them are real, a lot of it still isn't," David said.

Ellie spun the mug back and forth a few times on its saucer. "I made so many excuses for so long. I ignored so much. I have a colleague at Taconic who I trust dearly, I considered him a close friend and a good man. I told him about what happened that night. I recounted the entire story, shaking and crying through the hardest parts. At the end he told me I must have been hallucinating or dreaming. He told me things like that don't really happen, that it's against the laws of physics. I trusted him, and he made me feel small. The worst part of it is, a month ago if someone came into my office and told me that same story, I would've said the exact same thing he did. I would've brushed the person off." Ellie buried her head in her hands and stared down at the table.

David nodded and took a sip of his coffee. "I've been saying it for years. The stories people tell to each other matter. When someone recounts a story to another, there's something sacred in it. It's like a piece of their soul is chipped off and displayed out in the open, naked for everyone to see. People's lived experiences matter to me, they should matter to all of us. That's why I put your experience in my report, Ellie. Even though there isn't a shred of evidence to support it, I believe you."

"Amen to that," Charlotte said. She snapped her fingers like a celebrant at a beat poetry session.

Ellie smiled and met their faces. "Thank you, guys, it means a lot to me. Really. I just don't know what I'm going to do now. I'm a scientist, my life's work has been devoted to the natural world, but now I have to face the supernatural. It's like I've been blind and now I can see."

"I have an investigation coming up in a couple weeks at Ashwick Asylum. If you're up for it, I'd be happy to have you along." David finished off the last of his coffee.

Ellie shook her head. "I don't know if I want anything to do with paranormal investigations ever again."

"I understand."

Charlotte nudged David and flashed the face of her phone at him.

"Oh wow, we need to get on the road if we want Charlotte to make her flight." He scooted his chair away from the table.

Ellie stood to say goodbye.

"It was really great seeing you again before I fly home," Charlotte said. She wrapped her arms around Ellie in a cozy embrace. "I'll be back up this way again soon enough, and I won't forget to look you up when I get here." She glanced out the window at the falling flakes. "Maybe not until spring though."

"I'll just have to find a reason to come down to Lafayette before then," Ellie said.

PATRICK WALLACE

"Aren't *I* reason enough?" A sly grin crossed Charlotte's face.

David finished wrapping a scarf around his neck and reached out a hand to shake. Ellie took his firm grip and was reminded of the day she first met him in her office. "I hope to see you again soon, Ellie."

"Me too." Ellie released David's hand.

"Give Hux some love for me," Charlotte said as she and David made their way to the door.

"He gets plenty, but I'll give him a little extra for you anyway."

A bell rang as Charlotte and David opened the cafe door. They stepped out onto the sidewalk and disappeared into a flurry of falling snow.

Ellie sat down at the table and gathered her things. As she pulled a knitted cap on over her head, a busboy fumbled a mop. The wooden handle landed on the cafe's tile floor with a sharp crack. Memories bubbled from deep trenches in the vast sea of her mind. For a moment she tried to suppress them, to hide them away in a dark recess where they could fester and rot, but instead she let them come. She remembered the brutal and short life her mother had endured, she remembered her cruel and violent father, and she remembered Star's unconditional love and the comfort of his smell as she held him close.

Alone, at a small cafe table, tears came. They streamed down her cheeks, and Ellie buried her face in the palm of her hand to hide them. She sobbed quietly to herself and hoped no one in the cafe noticed her.

She accepted the horrors she had endured, both the

abuse she had suffered as a child and the unearthly entity she had encountered at Bruker House. She let the raw emotion flow over her. She lamented decades of pain, she wept for a stolen childhood, and she mourned for loved ones lost. She thought of Alaina and Julie, plucked from our reality into a world beyond.

Ellie hated herself for scoffing at Alaina's insight; the least she could do now was heed her advice.

Ellie stood and wiped her eyes dry with a napkin. She left it crumpled on the table alongside a smattering of dirty dishes and one small piece of the weight she carried. She left the cafe, her burden a hair lighter, and walked home in the wistful silence of falling snow.

Epilogue

B ruker House wallowed in its throne upon the hill. A light layer of snow blanketed the forest, a white world burning against the house's black soul.

The house stood unfettered by the elements, unburdened by the march of time. Within, walls were clean and square, fixtures pristine, its foundation solid. No leaks, no cracks, no blemishes betrayed decay. The scars it bore belonged not to the house itself, but to those who entered it.

For Bruker House carried no wounds. A wound is superficial, skin deep; a wound can heal. What festered within Bruker House reached deeper. The house was damaged, rotted, corrupted at the core. There would be no healing from the suffering it had endured, no recovery from the injuries inflicted upon it. No cleansing could ever undo that which had been done.

Deep within Bruker House, a dark heart beat, low and steady. What dwelt there waited for those who dared to test it. Those whose warmth it could not abide. Those that might be consumed.

ACKNOWLEDGMENTS

No book is written in a vacuum, and *Haunted* is no exception. There are countless people whose support I've depended on, without whom this novel would not have been possible.

Several incredible editors and proofreaders helped shape this work from a rough manuscript into a finished novel. Sarah LaPolla, Sean Leonard, and Raven Wilson. Without their talent and sharp eyes, the readers would be exposed to the raw, unfiltered machinations of my mind, and the world isn't quite ready for that yet.

Thank you Arlen Monroe, for creating the fantastic cover art, I couldn't be happier with how it turned out, and to Jen Greer, for somehow making me look good in my author photo.

To my parents, Lisa and Samantha. Anyone would be lucky to have such a supportive and loving family. Without you, I suspect I'd have amounted to nothing more than a burnout loser instead of the man I am today, a burnout loser with an advanced degree.

I'd like to thank Sarah Yandle, without her encouragement I'm not sure I would've had the confidence to start writing this book in the first place.

Of course, Juno, one of the greatest dogs of all time, who inspired the character of Hux.

Finally, my dog Tacoma. She'll never read this, but I think she understands how much she's loved. She saves me from the darkness every day.

COMING IN 2026…

A WHISPER

FROM

BEYOND THE VOID

AND OTHER STORIES

For news and updates visit
www.patrickwallace.com